"We should get better acquainted,"

Mike said, a boyish grin curving his mouth. "We've never really done anything together, not even when we were kids. We don't even know each other well."

Hallelujah, Callie cheered silently. Maybe he'd stop dismissing her as the sweet but annoying kid sister type. "At least you know I won't steal the silver," she teased.

"True."

To her amazement, Mike reached out and brushed errant strands of hair from her forehead. He was so close, Callie could smell the warm, masculine scent of him, and a piercing ache went through her body. She'd like to cuddle…feel welcome to slide into his arms and put her head on his chest.

She wanted to marry the man, for heaven's sake! Ever since she'd been a girl…

Callie, Get Your Groom—March 2000
Hannah Gets A Husband—May 2000
Jodie's Mail-Order Man—July 2000

Dear Reader,

March roars in in grand style at Silhouette Romance, as we continue to celebrate twenty years of publishing the best in contemporary category romance fiction. And the new millennium boasts several new miniseries and promotions... such as ROYALLY WED, a three-book spinoff of the cross-line series that concluded last month in Special Edition Arlene James launches the new limited series with A Royal Masquerade, featuring a romance between would-be enemies, in which appearances are definitely deceiving....

Susan Meier's adorable BREWSTER BABY BOOM series concludes this month with Oh, Babies! The last Brewster bachelor had best beware—but the warning may be too late! Karen Rose Smith graces the lineup with the story of a very pregnant single mom who finds Just the Man She Needed in her lonesome cowboy boarder whose plans had never included staying. The delightful Terry Essig will touch your heart and tickle your funny bone with The Baby Magnet, in which a hunky single dad discovers his toddler is more of an attraction than him—till he meets a woman who proves his ultimate distraction.

A confirmed bachelor finds himself the solution to the command: Callie, Get Your Groom as Julianna Morris unveils her new miniseries BRIDAL FEVER! And could love be What the Cowboy Prescribes... in Mary Starleigh's charming debut Romance novel?

Next month features a Joan Hohl/Kasey Michaels duet, and in coming months look for Diana Palmer, and much more. It's an exciting year for Silhouette Books, and we invite you to join the celebration!

Happy Reading!

Mary-Theresa Hussey

Mary-Theresa Hussey
Senior Editor

Please address questions and book requests to:
Silhouette Reader Service
U.S.: 3010 Walden Ave., P.O. Box 1325, Buffalo, NY 14269
Canadian: P.O. Box 609, Fort Erie, Ont. L2A 5X3

CALLIE, GET YOUR GROOM

Julianna Morris

Silhouette
ROMANCE™
Published by Silhouette Books
America's Publisher of Contemporary Romance

With grateful thanks to
Lana and the Alaska Division of Tourism
for sharing their knowledge and love
of the "Frontier State."

 SILHOUETTE BOOKS

ISBN 0-373-19436-6

CALLIE, GET YOUR GROOM

Copyright © 2000 by Martha Ann Ford

This edition published by arrangement with Harlequin Books S.A.

Visit us at www.romance.net

Printed in U.S.A.

JULIANNA MORRIS

has an offbeat sense of humor, which frequently gets her into trouble. She is often accused of being curious about everything…her interests ranging from oceanography and photography to traveling, antiquing, walking on the beach and reading science fiction. Choosing a college major was extremely difficult, but after many changes she earned a bachelor's degree in environmental science.

Julianna's writing is supervised by a cat named Gandalf, who sits on the computer monitor and criticizes each keystroke. Ultimately, she would like a home overlooking the ocean, where she can write to her heart's content—and Gandalf's malcontent. She'd like to share that home with her own romantic hero, someone with a warm, sexy smile, lots of patience and an offbeat sense of humor to match her own. Oh, yes…and he has to like cats.

IT'S OUR 20ᵗʰ ANNIVERSARY!
We'll be celebrating all year, continuing with these fabulous titles, on sale in March 2000.

Special Edition

#1309 Dylan and the Baby Doctor
Sherryl Woods

#1310 Found: His Perfect Wife
Marie Ferrarella

#1311 Cowboy's Caress
Victoria Pade

#1312 Millionaire's Instant Baby
Allison Leigh

#1313 The Marriage Promise
Sharon De Vita

#1314 Good Morning, Stranger
Laurie Campbell

Intimate Moments

#991 Get Lucky
Suzanne Brockmann

#992 A Ranching Man
Linda Turner

#993 Just a Wedding Away
Monica McLean

#994 Accidental Father
Lauren Nichols

#995 Saving Grace
RaeAnne Thayne

#996 The Long Hot Summer
Wendy Rosnau

Romance

#1432 A Royal Masquerade
Arlene James

#1433 Oh, Babies!
Susan Meier

#1434 Just the Man She Needed
Karen Rose Smith

#1435 The Baby Magnet
Terry Essig

#1436 Callie, Get Your Groom
Julianna Morris

#1437 What the Cowboy Prescribes...
Mary Starleigh

Desire

#1279 A Cowboy's Secret
Anne McAllister

#1280 The Doctor Wore Spurs
Leanne Banks

#1281 A Whole Lot of Love
Justine Davis

#1282 The Earl Takes a Bride
Kathryn Jensen

#1283 The Pregnant Virgin
Anne Eames

#1284 Marriage for Sale
Carol Devine

Chapter One

I'm late.

Michael Fitzpatrick cursed as he turned into the Kachelak airfield, gravel spinning beneath the wheels of his Dodge Dakota. Across the airfield he saw the small Cessna, and two people still standing in the plane's shadow.

A wry smile curved Mike's mouth. It was fairly obvious the pilot was flirting with the woman, and the woman was flirting right back. He'd have to warn his sister that Donovan Masters was an infamous ladies' man.

"Hey, sis!" he called, jumping from the Dakota and striding toward the couple. "Sorry I'm late. I got held up."

But it wasn't until Mike was within ten feet of the plane that he realized the diminutive female definitely *wasn't* his sister...not unless she'd shrunk several inches and colored her hair to a riotous chestnut.

"Oh, hi," the woman said, casually glancing at him as he approached. "Surprise. It's me, Callie."

Callie Webster? Mike shook his head. What was prim-and-proper Callie doing in Alaska? He circled around the wing...and suddenly his jaw dropped so hard it practically hit the airfield tarmac.

Prim-and-proper?

"Uh...Callie," he said stupidly, staring at the skimpy red tube top barely confining her breasts. A whole lot of creamy skin was exposed above and below that narrow band of red—which only seemed to draw attention to the lush curves within.

"Yup." She'd been leaning against the plane, but now she vaulted forward and threw her arms around his neck for a hug. "It's great to see you. Gosh, it's been a long while."

Automatically his arms had risen to catch her, and almost as instinctively he pushed her away. "Why are you dressed like that?" he demanded, then realized it wasn't any of his business. "The weather isn't warm enough to...er...need something so...cool."

"It's summer."

She shrugged her shoulders and he gulped. The tube top seemed glued in place, but that wasn't reassuring. And he wasn't the only one staring at Callie's bustline. Donovan was looking, as well. Mike ground his teeth—business partner or not, Donovan had better watch it. Callie and his sister had been friends all through childhood and he felt the same protective instincts for Callie that Elaine would have aroused in him.

Mike peeled off his outer flannel shirt and handed it to Callie. "Here. You'll be eaten by mosquitoes."

She slung the shirt over her arm. "Thanks, but I never get bitten," she said cheerfully.

His brown eyes narrowed in warning. "Callie, we have over twenty-five varieties of mosquitoes up here. Put the damn thing on."

"Why, Mike," she said, hurt tingeing her voice. "That isn't polite. You haven't even said hello."

"Hello. What are you doing here?"

Callie glanced at Donovan and shrugged again. "Mike and I grew up together—he's just like a brother. They're never glad to see you, either."

Donovan's face gleamed with amusement. "Don't pay him any attention. I'm delighted, and so is everyone else in the company. Mike doesn't count."

She grinned and a dimple appeared at the corner of her mouth. "You're sweet."

"Sure," Mike muttered. *Sweet* wasn't an appellation he would have attached to his partner, especially when it came to any female under ninety. As for Callie... He looked at her again, unable to believe his eyes. It wasn't just her clothing, it was the way she acted—confident and sexy and pretty damned sure of herself.

And she *still* wasn't wearing his shirt.

The last time he'd seen Callie Webster was over a year ago, on one of his rare trips home to Washington. Following their holiday tradition, the entire family had gone to the midnight candlelighting service on Christmas Eve. Callie had been playing the organ in a voluminous choir robe, with her long hair pulled into its customary braid.

The picture-perfect preacher's daughter.

After the service he'd said "hello," returned her quick hug, then promptly forgotten about her. After all, she was his sister's friend, and they'd both been a terrible nuisance when he was growing up. The fact that he'd gotten a lot closer to Elaine since reaching adulthood didn't change things.

"Callie," Mike said insistently—he needed to get some control back into the situation. "Where is Elaine?"

"Oh…" She waved her hand. "I realize she offered to be your office manager for the summer, but she's awfully busy. It isn't easy for her to just pick up and leave like that, you know."

"I know, but—"

"And since I didn't have any special plans for the summer, she asked me to take her place," Callie said, blithely disregarding the interruption.

"I see." A hint of Mike's reaction must have shown on his face, because she bristled.

"I'm perfectly capable of managing an office," she snapped.

"I'm sure you are," he said diplomatically. "But church work isn't the same as handling clients and taking cargo orders—or coordinating flight schedules and following up on billings, for that matter."

"I'll consider it a challenge." She tossed her head, sending her hair flying. Fiery strands covered her bare shoulders with a lacy pattern of light, and worse…it clung to her breasts, caught by static electricity to the red cotton knit. He groaned, hardly able to believe he was fixated—however briefly—on Callie Webster's body.

She was an innocent. A sweet kid who took care of her saintly father and taught Sunday school. She wouldn't be able to deal with their tough customers, or anything else in the air-transit business. Moreover,

Alaska wasn't an easy place to live, even in summer. He'd have to spend most of his time taking care of her.

Mike thought hard, trying to recall what Elaine had told him about Callie's sheltered life in Crockett. "But what will your father do? I know how much he depends on your help. He probably can't manage without you…or neither can the church, for that matter."

She didn't look concerned. "Pop is fine. And the church finally got enough money to renovate. With all the plaster dust and construction right now, they won't even miss me."

Besides, I don't plan on going back, Callie added silently. And blinked.

She couldn't tell Mike that she planned to stay in Alaska, could she? He'd run the opposite direction if he knew she wanted to get married. Of course, it wasn't very honest not telling him the truth.

I don't care, Callie told her conscience crossly.

If she couldn't vamp Mike, then she'd find someone else. She was tired of being the quiet, dutiful preacher's kid who behaved the way everyone expected. This was a new-and-improved Callie Webster. A woman of mystery. Bold. Provocative. Daring. A woman who knew what she wanted, and went out to get it.

Everybody knew Alaska was full of single men. It was an ideal place to change her image.

Right.

Mike wouldn't know what had hit him.

"I think Callie will be wonderful," Donovan said, warm approval in his tone and eyes.

"You *would*," Mike grumbled.

"Thanks," Callie said to Donovan, ignoring the

other man as though he were an irritating gnat. "We're going to get along great. I'm glad you picked me up in Anchorage—Mike probably would have left me at the airport."

"I aim to please, ma'am."

"Look, Callie, this won't work," Mike interrupted. "There's no place to stay in Kachelak. The motels are too expensive and there aren't any rentals."

Callie plastered an innocent look on her face. "But I thought Elaine was going to stay with you."

"Yeah. Well...that was the original plan. But you're not Elaine."

You'd better believe it, buster. She didn't intend to be treated like a bothersome kid sister. Not anymore. "I don't understand, I wouldn't be any trouble."

"That isn't the poin—"

"You can stay at my place," Donovan volunteered. He put an arm around her waist and smiled. His wolfish leer didn't fool Callie. Donovan was smart. He'd already sized up the situation and knew she was out for blood...*Fitzpatrick* blood to be exact, on a blood test for a wedding license.

And it was obvious he approved of the endeavor, which only went to show that dedicated bachelors thought marriage was just fine...for the other guy.

"That's a terrific solution." She glanced at Mike and shook with inward laughter. He appeared ready to explode. "Are you certain I won't be any trouble?"

"No trouble at all," Donovan assured. "It'll be my pleasure."

"No, it won't," Mike snarled. "She's staying with me."

Donovan shook his head, undaunted. "Now look, buddy. You didn't want Callie, and I do. You wouldn't want her to feel unwelcome when she's come all this way to help us out, would you?''

"It's not that I don't want her," Mike said, sounding so utterly frustrated that Callie almost felt sorry for him. "Of course I want her.''

Though it didn't mean anything…*romantic,* the words sent a pleasant warmth through her body. She'd had boyfriends before—she'd tried to put Mike out of her mind by dating other men. A long time ago she'd even gotten engaged, more out of affection and friendship than love. They would have had a good marriage, too, if Keith hadn't died in a car accident.

For an instant, regret dimmed Callie's excitement. She'd genuinely cared for Keith, only, there hadn't been any spark. No heat. Nothing to equal what she felt just thinking of Mike…and of the one time he'd kissed her.

Boy. It had happened the night of his college graduation, and he'd been so drunk, he didn't even remember that kiss. Callie pushed all distracting thoughts from her mind and hardened her heart. Vamps didn't let anything get in their way. They moved in and got what they wanted.

"You're kind to offer," she said with seeming reluctance. "But I'd better stay with Donovan.''

"No, you won't." Mike split a glare between them that could have fried eggs. "You're my responsibility. Where is your luggage?''

"Well…okay. It's in the plane.''

Muttering beneath his breath, he collected the three suitcases she'd brought and stomped toward his vehicle.

"That was gracious," Callie murmured reflectively. "I hope he remembers I go along with the luggage.''

Donovan chuckled. "Poor guy. He doesn't have a chance, does he?"

"Why, Mr. Masters, I don't know what you're talking about."

"Sure."

They watched as Mike threw the suitcases in the back of the Dakota with more force than necessary. Then he slammed shut the truck door and leaned against the fender, impatiently tapping his foot. Callie swallowed.

What had she talked herself into?

Michael Fitzpatrick wasn't a boy anymore. The muscled lines of his tall body were from hard work. His hair was still brown, though she'd detected a few threads of silver. For a moment, uncertainty filled her, because Mike was more like a stranger than a friend. For all her talk of growing up together, the three years separating them made a big difference.

She was thirty-one now. Hardly a kid. Mike was thirty-four. High time he got married and started a family. High time *she* got married and started a family. She just needed to find out if they were going to be the two halves of a single equation. It was one thing to fantasize about the boy you'd grown up loving, and quite another to discover if you still loved the man he'd become.

It hadn't seemed so urgent until she'd turned thirty; then she'd started imagining being alone the rest of her life. No kids. No husband. *No Mike.* When the trip to Alaska had come up she'd leapt at the opportunity.

"Here goes nothing," she mumbled, squaring her shoulders and heading toward the truck.

"You can still stay with me," Donovan offered.

"Separate beds?" she teased, comfortable with the

charming pilot in a way she'd never been comfortable
with Mike. Love and sex appeal certainly complicated
relationships.

"Only if you insist."

She laughed and kept walking.

Mike watched Callie smiling and flirting with Donovan and he clenched his fists. It wasn't his concern
if she wanted to get burned. But he'd warn her about
the risks, the same way he'd warn Elaine.

"I'll see you tonight," she called back, waving
goodbye to the other man.

"Six sharp. Don't dress, unless you think it's absolutely necessary," Donovan replied with a wink.

Mike growled. He actually heard it, rumbling from
his chest. *A date?* She'd already made a date?

"You're going out with him? I thought you came
to manage the office," he said when she reached the
Dakota. "To help us out. Our regular manager is having a baby, so she can't come in when you're not
available."

"Yes." A catlike smile curved her lips.

"Yes, what?"

"Yes, I came to manage the office, but it isn't a
twenty-four-hour-a-day job. I can manage a little so-
cializing between shuffling papers."

Mike sighed. They both knew managing the Triple
M office required more than shuffling some paper.
Callie was getting back at him for doubting her ability.
Hell, at least she was better than nothing. They'd got-
ten the office into a real tangle since losing Delia, and
now Delia was hinting she wouldn't return at all.

That's what getting pregnant did to a woman. They
wanted to stay home and take care of their kids, and

never mind the desperate men they deserted. Maybe it wouldn't matter someplace else, but it wasn't easy finding a replacement in Kachelak. That was one of the drawbacks of establishing their headquarters away from the higher-population centers, like Fairbanks or Anchorage.

"Never mind," he said, opening the door of the Dakota for Callie. "I was just trying to warn you about Donovan. He's a confirmed bachelor."

"No kidding?"

Mike walked around to the driver's side of the vehicle. "This isn't a joke, Callie. Donovan's a great guy, but as soon as he thinks you're serious he'll be out the door faster than you can blink."

"Oh?" She lifted one delicate eyebrow. "Who's to say *I* won't be the one out the door?"

In the process of fastening his seat belt, Mike gaped. Callie sounded serious, as though she engaged in light-hearted affairs all the time. Which he knew wasn't true. That is, he was pretty sure it wasn't true. She couldn't get away with acting uninhibited, not in Crockett, Washington. Crockett was a nice little town, but it certainly wouldn't tolerate the preacher's daughter running around with a lot of different men. Besides, she wasn't that kind of woman.

So he told her so.

"What did you say?" she gasped, sparks leaping from her green eyes.

"I said you weren't that kind—"

"I know what you said. For your information, I've had plenty of men interested in me. You're insulting. Just because my father's a preacher, that doesn't make me the antidote to romance."

How the hell *had he gotten into this?*

"I didn't mean to say you weren't desirable," Mike soothed. Her glare indicated she wasn't soothed, or even mildly appeased. "But you're...uh...a nice girl."

"Nice? That tears it. I'm staying with Donovan. Nobody calls me nice."

Mike took a deep breath. "That was a compliment...and you're *not* staying with Donovan."

"Some compliment. How would you like me to say you're a nice man?"

The question threw him. Certainly, it was death to a man's ego to be called *nice.* Nice was boring. Nice was a sucker's description. As soon as a woman called a man "nice," he could hear the death knell coming. A man wanted to be big, bad and a little dangerous.

Not nice.

Damn. He'd never imagined a woman would feel the same way, especially Callie.

"Okay, you're not nice." Now *that* hadn't come out right, either, and he could guess what she'd say about his awkward attempt to apologize.

"Thank you."

Contrary to his expectation, she sounded genuinely pleased and Mike rolled his eyes. Women. He was better off with his planes and the grumpy old moose who fed behind his house every evening.

"Shouldn't you show me the office?" Callie asked as he started the engine. "It's located here at the airfield, isn't it?" Despite her question, she yawned and settled back against the seat, closing her eyes as she did so.

He hesitated. They really needed a warm body occupying the office—to answer the phone if nothing else—but her flight had left Seattle at one-thirty the previous morning. Under the circumstances he wouldn't have expected Elaine to jump into work immediately, and the same applied to Callie. On the other hand, it would be nice to have an excuse to put off the inevitable. Callie living in his house? It gave him a queasy sensation of looming catastrophe.

"I'll show you the office tomorrow. You probably need some sleep," Mike said finally. *Before your date,* he added in his mind. Sheesh, that really irritated him. Donovan should have shown some consideration for their new employee.

Employee? Yeah, that's how he could treat Callie. Like an employee, even if she wasn't. Not really. She was doing a favor for Elaine, which translated into a favor for him. Still, it was all very disturbing.

"Callie?" he said.

She opened her eyes. "Hmm?"

"Why didn't someone phone me? To explain you were coming instead of Elaine?"

"It was all decided at the last minute. Besides—" her sleepy smile flashed at him "—we thought you'd get all blustery and say no."

Of course I'd say no, Mike growled inside his head.

He would have guessed Elaine's game right off… namely, that his baby sister was trying to fix him up with Callie. The thought made him wince. He didn't want to get married. He spent most of his time away from home, flying cargo or tourists around the state. A free and easy life, that's what he wanted—no wife nagging him, asking why he wasn't home when the plumbing burst or the kids got the measles.

Mike killed the engine and twisted in his seat. "Look, Callie. I think Elaine is trying to do some matchmaking."

A knowing grin curved her lips. "Of course she is, but don't worry about it. I'll keep out of your way, and you keep out of mine."

"Then you're not..." He paused, unsure of how to phrase his question.

"I might look for a husband," Callie said thoughtfully, "but you're safe." She yawned again and wiggled in her seat, making him aware of every inch of exposed skin above and below that ridiculous tube top. "Elaine can plot all she wants. That doesn't mean we have to go along. I mean really, the two of us together? It's absurd."

His brows drew together in a scowl. Everything Callie was saying should make him feel reassured and comfortable with her. Only, it didn't.

"Why absurd?"

She chuckled and curled her legs beneath her. "I don't know...you're six-two and I'm five-four. We'd look silly together. Besides, we've known each other forever. No thunderbolts here."

Her lingering smile annoyed him even more. How could she say that? They'd barely spoken since he'd moved north. After college a few hurried hellos and goodbyes were the sum of their so-called friendship since he'd left home. There hadn't been time for thunderbolts.

Not that he was interested. His curiosity was purely academic. Actually...his curiosity was masculine—no guy liked to be dismissed by a woman, no matter what the situation might be.

All at once Callie gave herself a little shake and sat up. "Now that we have that settled, I was wondering... You made it sound as though I won't have any time off. This isn't a seven-day-a-week job, is it?"

"Er...no." He relaxed. "Unless there's an emergency, you'll have a standard schedule—five days on, two off."

"Oh, good. I want to do some sightseeing, maybe even climb a glacier. And I understand there's a lot of hiking around here...even in the immediate area. Do you think I'll see any grizzlies? I'd love to see a polar bear in the wild, but I guess they're only around the Arctic ice cap. I'll have to go farther north to see them."

Subtle tension crept back into Mike's body. Why couldn't his sister have come instead of Callie? Elaine wasn't curious about fifteen-hundred-pound bears, and she'd been to Alaska often enough that sightseeing wasn't a high priority.

"You shouldn't go hiking by yourself," he said shortly. "It isn't safe."

"I wasn't planning to go by myself."

Mike sighed. "I don't have time for hiking, Callie."

"That's not a problem...you weren't invited."

Her obvious lack of interest made the rejection all that more stinging, though why he felt rejected he couldn't have said. He glanced at her as he started the engine. While visibly sleepy, she gazed eagerly at the scenery as they pulled onto the gravel road that led into town.

Mike cleared his throat. It was pointless to be so unsettled. This was good old Callie, even if she did look like a beach babe from sunny California. "We don't have any hiking clubs, kiddo. And the tours are pretty expensive."

"I don't need any tours." She gave him a sunny smile, apparently forgiving him. "Donovan is taking me to the Kenai Wildlife Refuge and—"

"Tonight?" Mike almost stomped on the brake so he could shake some sense into her. "You didn't buy that line, did you? We might have longer hours of daylight up here, but it's a long drive down and you couldn't possibly visit the refuge so late."

"Of course not," Callie said patiently. "We're going on the first day we're both available. Tonight we're just going to dinner."

Mike grunted.

She patted his arm. "Not feeling well?"

"I'm fine."

"That's good. Anyway, Travis Black said he loves hiking and he'll follow me anywhere. But I think he was just being polite."

Another line, Mike thought sourly, though Travis *was* an expert wilderness guide. "How did Travis get into this?"

"On the radio. He asked Donovan to describe me, and when Donovan said I had buck teeth and was wrinkled like a walrus, Travis immediately offered his services in showing me around. I don't think he believed Donovan about the teeth."

I wouldn't, either.

Donovan had been protecting his turf—one look at Callie's skimpy tube top and he'd gotten the complete wrong impression about her. But while Mike couldn't do anything about his two partners' social calendars, he could certainly ensure Travis's days off didn't coincide with Callie's. Travis wasn't a partner—not yet.

"Of course, Ross McCoy offered to fly me across Prince William Sound so we can climb Worthington Glacier. That'll probably be a two-day trip," she mused. "But he said he knows a nice place we can stay in Valdez."

"Really?" Mike felt the urge to loosen his collar, when all he was wearing was a black T-shirt. "When did you talk to Ross? The radio?"

Ross was his other partner in the business—a great guy, but not for a homebody like Callie. Besides, Ross had gotten burned by his ex-wife and had avoided women ever since. He definitely wasn't interested in getting married.

Callie bit her lip to keep from laughing. *Poor Mike.* He didn't look at all happy. "I met Ross in Anchorage. He was taking a load of fresh veggies to Nome, so he stopped by to say hi. I like Ross. He's really cute and he's awfully charming."

"I hadn't noticed."

"That's because you're not a woman. He said I could go to the Arctic Circle on one of his junkets. We might even land on the ice floe so I can get some pictures of polar bears."

"Terrific. Sounds like you're all set." Mike sounded quite disgruntled and she hid another smile.

"Yeah, I'm going to have a great time. At least Donovan and Ross and Travis are glad I'm here, even if you're not."

"They think they can get away with more...that I'll let them because you're not my sister."

Callie stretched languidly, aware of Mike's long sideways gaze. For the first time in her life she felt entirely feminine and sexy.

"You worry too much. They won't get away with anything I don't want them to."

"Oh? How much is that?"

She mused for a moment. "Enough, Mike. Enough."

"I see."

From the iron set to his jaw, Callie didn't think he liked her answer very much...which pleased her to no end.

Chapter Two

Enough?

What did she mean by that?

Remembering Callie's old-as-Eve smile, Mike was afraid he knew. She hadn't come to catch him as a husband; she'd come to spread her wings. It was natural, really. He'd never realized it before, but Callie was rather attractive. And thirty-odd years of living in Crockett as "the preacher's daughter" would have been frustrating for anyone.

Swell. Now he'd have to spend his summer making sure she didn't do something he knew she'd regret. It was instinctive to protect her. Even the toughest kids in Crockett had watched their mouths around Callie. He'd seen street toughs pummel their buddies for stepping out of line around Preacher Webster's daughter.

Don't say that. She's holy, you jerk.

And there was Callie...looking utterly disgusted at being called holy.

Mike had to grin, remembering those days. He'd

done it, too, cleaning up his language, making sure nobody stepped out of line with little Callie, and lumping her into the same category as kid sisters who were more trouble than they were necessarily worth.

He could strangle Elaine for doing this to him. He'd phoned her right after getting back to the house, and received an innocent "I don't know what you're talking about. Callie is doing us both a favor. And this way she gets to see part of Alaska."

Favor?

Right. His baby sister was matchmaking and he didn't want any part of her little plan. Of course…it *was* nice that Callie could have a trip. She probably didn't get a chance to travel very much.

Sighing, Mike continued working. He'd been cutting the next winter's supply of firewood before leaving to meet Elaine…and getting Callie instead. He would have flown to Anchorage himself, but Donovan had been returning from a hop to Fairbanks, so it hadn't made sense to make an extra trip. Now he wished he'd gone. He could have turned Callie around and put her on a flight back to Seattle. But no, instead she was here, taking a nap in one of his bedrooms.

Mike positioned a section of log on the chopping block and lifted his ax. It took a lot of wood to get through an Alaskan winter, though the weather wasn't as harsh in Kachelak as it was farther north.

Thwunk.

The piece split in two, one of which was still too large to fit into the woodstove. He took the larger half and positioned it again, wishing his other problems were so easily solved.

Sending Callie back to Seattle still seemed desirable, except there wasn't much hope of replacing their office manager. Kachelak was a great location, but the population was small and already dedicated to their own pursuits; individuality flourished in the frozen north.

He'd jokingly suggested that one of his partners get married and solve their labor dilemma that way. They hadn't been amused, since they felt the same about marriage that he did.

He swung the ax down.

Thwack.

The wood divided neatly and Mike tossed the two pieces onto a pile, then heaved another log to the block. He hammered a wedge into the grain and used a maul to do the initial split. The physical effort of cutting firewood usually helped focus his thoughts. Only, it wasn't helping this afternoon.

Callie Webster in a tube top.

His mind still had trouble working around that one. It was blasted inconvenient having her stay in his house. A sister was one thing, an unrelated woman was another. He'd have to watch his mouth, put the lid down on the toilet and be pleasant in the morning.

Mike hated mornings.

He'd rather fly through an ice fog than get up and talk to anyone before 10:00 a.m. On the other hand, Callie probably made delicious coffee. She belonged to that incomprehensible species who rose at the crack of dawn and loved it. And from what Elaine had said, she was a terrific cook, one of her specialties being caramel pecan pancakes.

Caramel pecan pancakes sounded very tasty, and they'd be even better for dinner, than breakfast. Maybe having Callie stay at the house wouldn't be so bad. Lately he'd gotten real tired of his own cooking.

* * *

Callie stepped onto the porch off her bedroom and took a deep breath. The air was fresh, redolent with the scent of the sea and whispering hemlock forests.

Soon after they'd arrived, Mike had gone outside to work, muttering something about her taking a nap. She'd watched him chopping wood from the kitchen window…all masculine grace and power, muscles working fluidly beneath skin slicked with sweat. She still heard the solid thunk and whack of the ax striking, and Callie moaned softly, a restless ache in her breasts and stomach.

Don't think about it.

Right. Like it was possible to think about anything else. She ought to be asleep, but her mind was too active. And her body… She shivered.

Mike always did that…made her feel things, hot and fast, spinning inside like a whirling top. Inevitably Callie had compared every man to him. They'd always come up short.

"Open your eyes, Michael Fitzpatrick," she breathed. "You never really came back, so I came to you."

Finally.

Everything had finally come together like the pieces to a murder mystery—means, motive and opportunity. And a dash of courage, because she'd been raised with the traditional idea that a woman didn't chase a man; she waited demurely until he noticed her.

Blying Sound glimmered in front of the house, which was perched high above the water out of sight from the town. It was a lovely place—the house old and solidly built, with at least five bedrooms.

Perfect for a family.

Callie smiled and leaned on the railing. Cool air brushed her arms and bare midriff, reminding her of Mike's reaction to the provocative outfit.

"Serves him right," she murmured.

It was about time he saw her as a woman, though the tube top might have been a little much. She'd shocked herself when she bought it. Maybe it wasn't any more revealing than a bikini, but she'd never worn a bikini, either.

She'd expected to blush like crazy the first time she was seen in public, yet it hadn't worked out that way. The unadulterated male attention had been worth every embarrassed prickle. Not that she wanted to dress like that all the time—just for special occasions.

It had taken her a long time to reach this point. Years of being the sweet-little-girl-next-door, of feeling guilty because she'd never loved Keith the way he deserved. She'd been cast in the role of a tragic, grieving not-quite-a-widow, returned home to care for her father because she had nothing else to live for. Her grief had been genuine, but not the shattering devastation her friends and family supposed.

Another yawn widened her mouth and she strolled inside to inspect the big, comfortable bed. Maybe she should try to sleep. She wanted to look her best for her date with Donovan. Mike mustn't suspect she had anything on her mind but having a great time with his partners in Triple M Transit.

Besides, if nothing else, she *was* going to have a great time. They were terrific guys—Mike wouldn't have gone into business with them if they weren't.

Still, Mike was her reason for coming to Alaska, and she was gambling a lot on the plot she and Elaine had hatched—her heart most of all.

* * *

It was late in the afternoon when Mike sank his ax into the chopping block and decided to call it quits. Summer in Kachelak was pleasantly mild at best, yet perspiration had soaked his hair and body from the long hours of work.

Stopping at the refrigerator, he grabbed a bottle of iced tea and took a long swallow, then stuck his head under the faucet in the sink. Though chilly, it felt good. He scrubbed his upper body, sluicing water over his arms and chest.

"Mike?"

He jumped, bumping his head on the tap and swearing under his breath.

Jeez, he'd almost forgotten about his "houseguest." A memory of round curves, faithfully outlined by fire-engine-red cotton, rose instantly before his eyes and he groaned. Well, he hadn't exactly *forgotten*. But it was tough, reconciling his lifelong image of Callie with the woman who'd hugged him at the airport.

The clothes were a shock, yet the hug had been all Callie. Sweet, affectionate Callie, with the softest heart on the West coast, though as a kid he'd thought it was dumb and disgustingly mushy.

"Mike?" she called again. "Are you here?"

"In the kitchen." He turned the water off and wiped his face with a dishcloth before turning around. Callie was standing in a pool of gold sunlight only a few feet away. "My God, what the hell are you wearing?" he demanded harshly, forgetting his earlier resolve to watch his mouth around her.

"A dress."

"That isn't a dress. It's another tube top," he snapped, slapping the towel onto the counter.

She ran the palms of her hand over the clinging black knit. Like the red top, it stayed in place with some kind of invisible magic—no straps, just a sheath of black that exposed her shoulders and a startling expanse of silky thigh encased in sheer black stockings.

"You're exaggerating," Callie said, undaunted by his frown. "This is a very stylish dress."

"Take it off."

Her eyebrows lifted. "I don't think that's a good idea. Donovan said I didn't have to dress, but I'd rather have clothes on when he gets here. I don't want him getting the wrong impression."

"I..." To his amazement, heat crawled up Mike's neck and he gritted his teeth. "That's not what I meant. Go put on something else."

"Why?"

Why?

What a dumb question.

His gaze traveled over the black "dress." The fabric was so soft that anything beneath it would be outlined—like the lacy edge of a bra or panties. And except for a faint line about her waist, it was perfectly smooth, which meant she was only wearing those stockings. Mike broke out in another sweat.

No bra. No slip. *No panties.*

Though she still seemed to be waiting for an answer, Callie opened the refrigerator and bent over, examining its contents. Mike's lungs froze as he imagined what he'd see if the skirt inched up another two inches. Or what Donovan might see...and touch.

Damn. He was losing his mind and it was all Callie's fault. He'd been handed a stick of dynamite to protect. Why weren't her brothers here, guarding her virtue? It wasn't his job, yet he was stuck with it just the same.

"Do you mind if I have some milk?" she asked, straightening and holding up a carton.

"Sure. After you put on something decent."

"This is decent," she said coolly.

"It's trashy," Mike shouted furiously.

"Why you narrow-minded chauvinist *jerk*," Callie hissed. "You'd think it was perfect if your date wore a dress like this, but it's unacceptable for *me*. What a stupid double standard. I won't be ordered around, not by you or anyone else."

Mike already regretted his rash words. He knew better than to insult a woman's clothes. And Callie didn't look trashy; that was the problem. With her rich abundance of chestnut hair and that creamy complexion she looked like a dream. Classy and sultry at the same time—a combination unsettling to his stomach.

"I'm sorry," he mumbled. "I didn't mean that. But your father—"

"I'm thirty-one, Mike," Callie said curtly. "Not a child. My father wouldn't think of telling me what clothes to wear."

"Yeah, but…"

Callie's high heels clicked on the floor as she walked to the cupboard she'd examined earlier. She took down a glass and tried to control her temper. At the moment she was reconsidering the plot she'd hatched with Elaine.

Get married to Michael Fitzpatrick?

Right now she didn't care if he dropped off the face of the earth, never to be seen again.

Trashy.

Ugh.

He had a lot of nerve. Was he forgetting she'd seen the type of girl he'd dated in high school? Granted, teenage boys weren't usually attracted to "good" girls—and by all accounts his tastes had improved since then—but that wasn't the point. If she went stark naked, it wouldn't make her trashy. That came from the type of person you were.

"For your information," she said, pouring the milk, "Elaine has practically this same dress, only it's royal blue. She wore it to your parents' thirty-fifth wedding anniversary party two years ago. I don't recall you throwing a fit over *her* looking trashy."

"I don't remember."

From the expression on Mike's face, she knew he was lying.

"Really?" Callie prompted. "You said she looked great. And my dad thought she looked charming. You seem to be more judgmental than he is."

"I said I was sorry," he muttered. "You don't have to rub it in."

Callie had every intention of rubbing it all over him. He wanted to keep seeing her as the prim preacher's daughter, not as a woman. But she was unmistakably dressed like a woman, so she didn't fit into the neat little role he'd cast for her to play...just like everyone else in Crockett. It was hard enough exploring the real Callie without him fighting her every step of the way.

She took a swallow of milk. "I just want things to be clear between us."

"How clear would you like them to be?"

Mike crossed his arms over his stomach and stared at her grimly. His shoulders were broad, tanned and intimidating. A dark whorl of hair descended down his chest, narrowing until it was a thin line, disappearing beneath the top button on his jeans. Abruptly the muscles in Callie's throat had trouble working, so she set the glass on the counter.

"You're not my brother, Mike. And I stopped needing a guardian a long time ago."

From the flicker of his eyes she knew she'd hit pay dirt. As long as he could object to her clothing like a brother, he was safe. He didn't have to see her as anything but his sister's friend—the preacher's daughter who was expected to act and dress in a certain fashion.

Criminy. Mike had moved away from Crockett sixteen years ago to attend college and he *still* had the same ideas as the ninety-year-old widow who always sat in the same pew every Sunday. This was going to be even tougher than she'd thought, and a flutter of uncertainty hit her, stronger than before.

The sound of a vehicle driving up the hill only increased the tension in the air.

Callie drew a deep breath. "That must be Donovan. I'd better go out to meet him."

"Yeah."

"Don't wait up for me."

A bleak, frustrated anger filled his eyes. "Not a chance, doll."

"Well...I'll see you tomorrow."

"Whatever."

Mike watched Callie leave, feeling like the ground had been ripped from under his feet. He didn't know the woman who had just walked out of his house. She was a stranger in a black dress, high heels, and scented with the seductive fragrance of an expensive perfume.

Her legs couldn't be as long as they looked—her head didn't even reach the top of his shoulder. She had a body that wouldn't quit, fiery green eyes and a set of wonderfully kissable lips.

A stranger.

"God, I'm losing it," Mike muttered and grabbed his tea, draining the bottle. For the first time in his life he really needed a drink. He tried to remember if there was any alcohol in the house. Not being much of a drinker, he couldn't remember.

None in the pantry.

And none in the refrigerator—not even beer. Mike slammed the door shut and scowled. A vision of Callie bending over and searching the interior made him choke. He backed away from the appliance.

Wait a minute.

He still had the bottle of Glenfiddich Scotch Ross had given him for his birthday. It was a shame to use fine whiskey for the sole purpose of getting smashed, but what the hell—it was medicinal.

The last time he'd gotten drunk was the traditional blowout after college finals. His *last* finals. Graduation. Freedom from cracking the books. Sometime in the middle of that evening he'd kissed the hottest girl on the face of the earth. He couldn't remember her name, her face or where she'd come from, but he remembered that kiss.

That's why he hadn't gotten drunk since. Too many questions. Too much wondering if she was as hot as he'd thought, or if it was an alcohol-induced fantasy. A fantasy lady for a fantastic kiss.

Mike dropped onto the couch in his living room and poured himself a shot of the Scotch. He wasn't "waiting up" for Callie, he was just enjoying a pleasant drink as he watched the view. He'd paid a lot for that view and was entitled to watch it anytime he wanted.

For that matter, Callie had been awfully impressed with the entire house.

His eyes narrowed. She'd made it clear she didn't want his protection, but if she came in crying, he'd make Donovan pay.

Hours later Mike was still "not waiting up." The sun had set shortly after 10:00 p.m. They hadn't reached the summer solstice yet, but it wouldn't be long. A wide yawn split his mouth and he realized he was dead tired. They'd been pulling double shifts lately, trying to cover the office and fly and run the business at the same time.

"Mike, why are you sitting in the dark?" Callie asked from behind him.

The question made him jerk upright. He'd fallen asleep and hadn't heard her come in. Mike lifted the bottle and blinked at it. Almost full. That's right, he'd only had two drinks. Unfortunately the alcohol had gone straight from an empty stomach to his weary head.

"Just watching the view, doll."

"In the dark?"

He tried to shake himself wider awake, but his brain wouldn't cooperate. "I'll do it my way, and you do whatever you want. That's what you said, isn't it?"

"Actually…I said we should keep out of each other's way." Callie switched a table lamp on and he sighed. While it was dim, the extra light hurt his head, and he wasn't too tired to ignore the exhilaration in her eyes, or the mussed condition of her hair.

She certainly wasn't crying, so he wouldn't have to kill Donovan after all.

Even if he wanted to.

Callie had certainly flung him into a highly illogical

state. Of course, women had been doing that to men for thousands of years; why should anything be different now?

"Turn that off," he ordered. And to his complete astonishment, she complied.

"Have a little to drink?" she asked.

"Just a little, and it's quality Scotch, not a bender," he said defensively, though she didn't seem offended. "I'm just tired."

"I know. Elaine says you hardly drink at all."

Had his sister volunteered that information, or had Callie asked? For some reason Mike liked the idea of Callie keeping tabs on him. She'd always been a nice person.

Nice...? *Wrong.* His brows drew together. She didn't want to be called nice. "Did you have a good time?" he asked, keeping his tone neutral.

"The best." Callie sat on the end of the couch and tucked her feet beneath her. "The northern lights were really wild. Donovan said it was unusual this time of year, so he took me up in his plane to see them better. We opened the windows up and the wind blew in.... It was incredible." She laughed and shook her hair across her shoulders. "I'm all tangled, but it was worth every minute."

Hmm. Mike felt better. At least Donovan had kept his hands to himself for that part of their date—even Donovan had never mastered the art of flying a Cessna with his feet.

"I hope you wore a coat. It gets pretty cold up there." He yawned again and his eyelids drooped.

"Don't worry—I won't get pneumonia and deprive you of an office manager." The slight edge in her voice hinted she was still angry over their earlier "discussion."

"I'm not worried. You're a pal to help out."

Callie glared at Mike, getting provoked all over again. He'd been dopey and endearing, and she'd been almost ready to forgive being called trashy—*almost.* And now he was calling her a pal. She wasn't his pal. Why couldn't he simply see her as a desirable woman?

Maybe she could throw herself at him. Kiss him senseless. But that would be rather obvious. And it might ruin things altogether.

What if she got up and slipped on her high heels…? She could fall across him and see what happened.

Yeah, it was a possibility.

Callie stretched. "It's late. I'd better get some sleep so I can start work early. Donovan says the office is a horrible mess."

"Uh-huh."

Mike sounded awfully sleepy, so Callie put her hand on his leg to help herself upright. His eyes shot open.

"Yikes…" She laughed. "Sorry about that. I didn't realize how deep the couch was."

Trying to make her "fall" look good, Callie twisted her ankle as she tumbled over Mike, letting out a genuine yelp of pain.

That hurt, she informed herself. *I hope it was worth it.*

The bottle he'd been clutching clunked to the floor. "Are you okay?"

"Sure. I love bruising my dignity."

His chest rumbled with a chuckle and waves of heat rolled through Callie. Brother, this was disgusting. She got close to the man and her body went crazy. She hated acting like a spinster stereotype, but she *did* feel rapacious and love starved, especially sprawled all over him.

Mike's hands slid over her waist and Callie held her breath. He was going to push her away, do the gentlemanly thing and help her up.

Dammit.

Callie ruefully acknowledged her level of frustration with the mute curse. She didn't often swear, but when she did, it was for a good reason…or at least a *strong* reason.

But she gulped when Mike's hands closed over her bottom, hard and sensuous at the same time. She didn't say *anything*. Talking might bring him to his senses, and that was the last thing she wanted at the moment.

The unmistakable outline of Mike's arousal pressed into her abdomen, making her dizzy.

His hands seemed to be urging her up his body. She was glad to comply, especially when one of those hands reached up to stroke her face—strong fingers, combing through her hair, pulling her into a kiss.

Dear heaven…the moan from Callie's throat was lost in his mouth, drowned in the unique flavor of Mike and Scotch. *This* is what she'd been craving. Even when she'd succeeded in pushing him from her mind—sometimes for months at a time—she'd craved the excitement and passion of his embrace.

She straddled Mike's waist and stroked her tongue over his lips, an erotic invitation to deepen the kiss. It was instinctive, a knowledge born of hope and longing and feminine intuition.

He rewarded her urgency, his fingers rhythmically squeezing and releasing her bottom, intensifying the tremor spinning through her core. His tongue delved into the humid warmth inside her mouth, tracing the even edge of her teeth. Velvet on velvet, infusing their lungs with the other's breath.

Shaking violently, Callie finally tore away and collapsed on Mike's chest. She couldn't think, couldn't do anything but feel and taste him.

Taste and feel…

Callie moaned again, unable to resist exploring the muscled contours beneath her cheek. She tasted the saltiness of his skin, tracing the hard points of his flat nipples with her fingernails, and sensed a deep shudder rising from him. This wasn't her need alone, it was the mutual desire of two people who were surely meant to be together.

And then…she heard a quiet snore in her ear.

What?

She wanted to hit him. Passion was zinging through her veins and the dope was sound asleep.

Rat.

Louse.

Cretin. How could he fall asleep on her?

When she'd finally called him every insult available, Callie slid to the ground and drew her knees against her chest. She'd be glad in the morning that nothing happened, but it wasn't morning and she was hurting. Unrequited love was bad enough, but unrequited passion was physical torture…not that she should complain. More than one boyfriend had pointed out the discomforts of such a condition.

She wished she'd been more sympathetic.

Mike probably wouldn't remember this kiss, either. He'd been kissed by so many women, what was one more?

Callie scowled.

The northern lights still danced across the sky, spinning pink ribbons of light that eclipsed the stars. No wonder Mike loved Alaska so much. She'd love it, too, if she got the chance.

Right. Callie nodded. She hadn't grown up managing her family for nothing. Those skills must be good for something...like winding Mike around her little finger.

At the same time a sigh welled out of her chest. Mike wasn't easily convinced. By tomorrow he would have shored his defenses and she'd have to tumble them down again.

Well, too bad.

The trick was not letting him affect her so easily.

The ghostly lights continued to dance as Callie repaired her resolve. She might not succeed, but Michael Fitzpatrick was about to take one heck of a ride. Maybe along the way he'd discover his heart...and the girl he'd left behind.

Chapter Three

His neck hurt.

Mike opened sandpapery eyes and gazed blearily at his world. It didn't look right. Then he realized he was in the living room, rather than his bed.

It still didn't look right.

Damnation. He'd fallen asleep in the middle of talking to Callie. Yet, there was something else...a vague memory of Callie falling and landing on his chest.

He'd bet it was those idiotic spike heels she'd been wearing. They weren't safe, even if they did make her legs look a mile long. It had to be the heels doing that. Amazing what the right clothing could do for a person.

Mike raised his head and sniffed hopefully. A blanket had been solicitously tucked around him, but he smelled nothing resembling caramel pecan pancakes...or coffee, bacon or any other hint of domestic comfort coming from the kitchen.

Great, not only had he slept badly, but he'd have to make his own coffee.

"Callie?"

Silence reigned.

He climbed to his feet and stumbled to the kitchen. He needed a shower, a toothbrush and a bottle of aspirin. *And coffee most of all.* He'd fight one of Callie's polar bears for a cup of coffee.

"Hey, Callie?"

The kitchen was spotless except for a square of white paper on the counter, the corner weighted down with an empty bottle. He lifted the note and squinted at the letters.

Mike,
Ross is picking me up, and he offered the loan of a truck so I'll have my own transportation. Isn't that great of him?
Hope you feel better.

Callie.

First Donovan, and now Ross. Mike crumpled the note and tossed it into the sink. If they had their way, he'd never see the woman.

Don't forget Travis.

Yeah, he'd forgotten Travis. The expert in hiking, who'd follow Callie anywhere. It had to be a terrific boost to her ego, being chased by three different men...which left ol' Mike Fitzpatrick hanging around like a sore thumb to make sure she didn't get caught.

Damn Elaine and her schemes. He'd never interfered with *her* life...at least not very much. There was that louse she'd been dating in college whom he'd scared off, but she couldn't still be holding that against him, right? Okay, so the guy had made it big with some computer circuit doohickey and was now worth seven or eight figures. Big deal.

Mike rubbed his face and made a cup of coffee in the microwave. Peanut butter on toast would suffice for breakfast—it wasn't like he was used to anything else. Another morning of peanut butter wouldn't kill him.

By the time he'd showered and swallowed a handful of aspirin tablets, the morning looked a lot brighter. Maybe he'd wander down to the airport and take Callie to lunch. Looking at his watch, Mike amended that to dinner. It was the polite thing to do—he hadn't exactly been welcoming when she arrived. Besides, a few carefully directed words of warning might be all she needed to watch her step.

After all, he trusted his partners and employees...just not with Callie.

"I'll check the flight schedules and get back to you," Callie said into the phone, then set the receiver back in the cradle.

Her work was cut out for her—the office wasn't just a mess, it was a certifiable disaster area.

Callie looked around and plotted her next course of action. Both Ross and Donovan had said she had carte blanche to change things to her satisfaction.

What would they say to a bulldozer?

It might be her only prayer.

Their former office manager obviously had a higher tolerance for grunge than she did. An ancient typewriter and adding machine vied with empty oil cans, engine parts, cargo orders and billing receipts. Boxes—containing everything from an unused computer to a bundle of girlie magazines—were stacked haphazardly throughout the cluttered space.

Actually, the magazines had been already removed. *Hastily.* To the red-faced embarrassment of both men, with a fumbling explanation that it was popular in the bush areas of Alaska.

What? Did they think she'd never heard of adult magazines? Men were so predictable.

Callie made some notations on a pad of paper. She needed to tell Mike to keep quiet about her father being a preacher. A lot of guys treated her different when they knew—as though she'd already been fitted for a halo and was headed for a nunnery.

Yuck.

The sight of a blue Dodge Dakota being parked outside lifted her spirits. It was about time Mike showed up—she'd been hard at work since 7:00 a.m.

"Callie?"

"Is that you, Mike?" She bent over the desk, scribbling furiously on her pad. It wouldn't be smart to let him think she'd been waiting for him, wondering if he'd remember a certain sizzling kiss....

"Of course it's me. Who were you expecting?"

You...of course. "How are you feeling?" she asked, watching him from the corner of her eye. "You were sound asleep when I left this morning."

"Asleep? Try unconscious." Mike grinned wryly, showing his sense of humor hadn't been impaired by a night on the couch. "Honest, that was completely out of character. I only had two drinks...but they didn't sit well on an empty stomach."

"I know," Callie said. Disappointment warred with relief in her chest. Mike was too comfortable, sliding into his joking mode. He probably didn't remember kissing her.

"Good." He sat on a stack of boxes and looked around. "Say, this place looks better already. I'm impressed."

You should be, buster. Callie had no illusions. Mike saw her as an appendage of her father, better equipped to organize ice cream socials than run an office. He had no idea she'd created a small but successful business as a management consultant. As she'd told Elaine, *let Mike find out the hard way.* Meaning, she wanted to see how far he'd stick his foot in his mouth.

"I'm just getting started," she murmured. "But I almost had heart failure when I got here. How can someone who's so meticulously neat at home be such a slob at work?"

A dull red crept under Mike's tan. "Things got out of control. It's been a rough month without Delia."

"Oh, yeah?" Callie found a pencil and used it to lift a greasy black *something* from the desk blotter. "It took longer than a month to become so disreputable. This is a long-term condition—I only hope it's treatable."

He snatched the whatever-it-was and threw it into the wastebasket. "Delia never minded."

"Delia must be a saint. I, however, am not. Frankly, I think she got pregnant as an excuse to bail on you guys."

She lifted the stained blotter and sent it sailing through the window. After a couple runs to the exterior Dumpster, she'd taken to pitching everything through this convenient opening. Ross was servicing an engine in the maintenance hanger, and he periodically appeared to collect the discarded items.

When she turned around she saw Mike frowning. "What?"

"You're limping."

"I know." Callie grimaced. While her ankle wasn't badly injured, it was a pointed reminder she should think before acting. "I...uh, fell last night."

"Yeah, I kind of remember."

Wonderful. Did he "kind of" remember kissing her? This could get downright humiliating—a blow to her self-esteem, and she'd only been in Alaska for a day.

"These things happen," she mumbled.

"I should take a look," Mike announced, and promptly lifted her to the desktop, with her legs dangling over the edge. "We can't be too careful."

"I'm fine." But she wasn't, because her breathing got all erratic when he touched her. What about her resolve not to let him affect her so much?

"No, I'm responsible for your safety."

Mike sounded like a beleaguered great-uncle, so Callie considered kicking him in a vulnerable spot. But she sucked in her breath when he sat on the desk chair and put her sandal-clad foot in his lap. Thank goodness she'd shaved her legs. He removed the sandal and gently rotated her foot.

"Tell me where it hurts?" Mike asked, frowning now with concentration.

"Higher," she mouthed to his bent head. From recent personal experience she knew cold showers weren't everything they were cracked up to be, and they did nothing to make a particular kind of hurting go away. In fact, she'd climbed into the shower, cringing under the cold spray, and decided it was a totally ineffective remedy.

Aw...drat. Why couldn't Mike have developed a beer belly and disgusting personal habits over the past twelve years?

But *nooo*.

Despite his rough night, he'd shaved and put on a clean white shirt and jeans. And there wasn't an extra ounce on his flat stomach. Only...it wasn't just the way he looked that turned her inside out. It was the endearing grin that still warmed his face, the intelligence in his eyes and the way he made her feel. Those things hadn't changed, either.

"Callie?"

"It's fine," she protested halfheartedly. "Besides, you're not a doctor."

"No, but I'm an emergency medical technician. Sprained ankles are nothing—I've even delivered a few babies."

Her jaw dropped. Michael Fitzpatrick? The guy who'd grossed out over Marcus Welby, M.D., delivering a baby on television? *That* Michael Fitzpatrick? And why hadn't Elaine told her about this little development?

"Don't look so shocked," he drawled.

"Yeah, but you're... This is so weird."

Mike grinned, pleased he'd managed to finally shock Callie. Her poise and outrageous clothing had certainly startled him, and he wanted to return the favor.

"In this business it made sense to get some emergency training."

"I don't believe it." Callie leaned forward and he found his attention focused on the bodice of her sundress. The pale yellow fabric should have clashed with her not-quite-red hair, yet it didn't. It was a very nice dress—not nearly as shocking as the black one. Or maybe he was becoming shockproof.

Reluctantly his gaze dropped back to her ankle.

"You don't believe what?"

She shook her head. "Mike, you threw up when the cat had kittens. Did space aliens come down and suck your brain?"

Trust Callie to recall such an embarrassing detail of his childhood. He could only hope she'd keep quiet around his partners—no point in giving them something else to rib him about.

Mike rubbed her ankle and the arch of her foot. "I was a teenager. Callie...most of our towns are only accessible by plane. Even when a doctor is available, a little training can help save a life. Donovan and Ross are EMT's too."

"I see."

And Callie did see, though it made her uneasy.

Boys grew into men. They shouldered responsibility and changed. Mike really wasn't the same boy who'd kissed her when she was nineteen. Maybe his horizons had expanded beyond what she could offer him.

At heart she was still the preacher's daughter who'd never lived more than fifty miles from her hometown. Would Mike ever need her? Except for the organizational disaster in his "corporate" office, he seemed pretty self-sufficient. And anyone could fix the Triple M office, it didn't have to be Callie Webster.

No.

She couldn't think like that.

Callie closed her eyes for a second, gathering her self-confidence. Mike was the only guy who'd ever done this to her. She'd grown up in public relations; that was a big part of being a preacher's kid. Poise.

Aplomb. Organizational skills. Dishwasher hands…
yeah, there was an endless parade of dishes at church
dinners. She never had any trouble handling *those*
things, but Mike knocked her right off center. Perhaps
that's why she liked him so much.

"There's some swelling in this ankle, but it doesn't
seem too bad."

"That's what I said," she muttered.

Next time she'd just throw herself at Mike. Be obvious. She wouldn't stoop to ruses that left her with
an aching ankle…and aching everywhere else. *If* she
ever threw herself at him again. Right now, the possibility was a toss-up.

Mike patted her knee with an avuncular smile.
"You should probably take some aspirin for the swelling."

The smile stiffened her spine…and made her hungry for revenge. With a tight smile of her own, she
leaned over and retrieved a file from the center desk
drawer. And though she hadn't planned it, her sandal
grazed a particularly *personal* part of Mike's lap.

A bonus. Payback for treating her like a sweet-
cheeked child who didn't know how to come in from
the rain.

"It's good you're here," she said with efficient
crispness, ignoring the muscle ticking in his jaw. "I
have some questions I'd like to ask about the company. I don't want to make any mistakes."

"Sure." Mike dumped her into the chair he'd been
using, then backed off like he'd been burned. He
nearly fell over one of the stacks of boxes and had to
lunge to keep them from falling.

Callie bit her lip so hard, she drew blood. Laughing
would be highly impolitic.

"What can I tell you?" he asked, once the stack was righted and he'd cleared his throat.

"I haven't gotten very far, but I've found a lot of stray invoices, et cetera, that don't match up…that kind of thing."

"Uh-huh."

"Like this one, for example." She held up a grubby piece of paper. Mike just nodded. Clearly he didn't have any intention of getting close enough to read it. "It's for three crates of Spam, but the company only billed the customer for two."

"Oh, that. Spam is the only thing old man Austin used to eat, so we always brought in extra. He gave us a loan when we started business, so we tried to do him favors."

Callie made a small face. "What about fruits and vegetables?"

Mike grinned. "He wouldn't touch 'em."

"And he's dead now?"

"Yup…a polar bear ate him." The teasing glint in his face made her tingle. "Anything else you need?"

"Hmm." She fingered the slick paper of the magazine she'd hidden inside the file jacket. *Time for revenge.* "Do you have Delia's address? She left some reading material I think she might want."

"Yeah, well, it's around. I didn't know Delia liked to read—what is it?"

"Just this *Playgirl* magazine." Callie held the dog-eared publication in the air, letting the centerfold flop open.

"Callie!"

She hadn't practiced her innocent face for nothing. "Yes?"

"That's not… *Hell.*"

From the other side of the door she heard a groan. Ross McCoy, she decided. He must have been planning to come inside, then waited when he overheard the gist of the conversation. Smart guy. She appreciated that in a man.

Callie surveyed the amply endowed male model and shrugged. "He's not bad, except I prefer men with shorter hair—of course, his other qualities make up for a lot. But this guy is a lot more attractive." She flipped to another picture in the magazine and waved it in the air.

For a second Callie thought she'd gone too far. She wanted to get Mike's attention, not give him a heart attack. Then she heard a muffled crack of laughter and the door swung open.

"Better get out of here, pal," Ross advised his speechless partner. "Sometimes a strategic retreat is highly advisable...and this is definitely one of those times!"

Mike was chopping wood again. A lot of wood. At this rate he'd have enough wood for a dozen winters. He couldn't believe Callie had brazenly analyzed the picture of a naked male model without blushing.

Callie.

It was medieval of him, but in his heart of hearts he hadn't believed she'd ever seen a naked man.

None of it made any sense.

At the same time, he couldn't forget the mischievous laughter in her green eyes. Callie had known exactly what she was doing to him. At least...she knew part of what she was doing.

Mike swung the ax so hard, he split the log and buried the head deep in the cutting block.

"Damn," he muttered, working the blade free and lifting it again.

He kept remembering his inexplicable response to Callie. Why had he insisted on examining her ankle? She plainly wasn't seriously injured—a day or two and she'd be good as new. Yet, when her foot had accidentally brushed his groin... Mike groaned in the middle of swinging the ax, hitting the log sideways and sending a reverberating jolt through his body.

Enough. Mike dropped the handle and rubbed his tingling hands. At this rate he'd chop off one of his toes, or some other useful part of his anatomy.

So what if Callie had shocked him...*again?*

His life had been monastic for the past year, so it was natural he'd responded to her touch—an involuntary male reaction. It didn't mean anything. The few single women they had in Kachelak were looking for husbands, not carefree flings. Short, fat, tall...it didn't seem to matter what the guy looked like. They wanted a ring on their finger and lots of babies. *Babies.* Jeez, didn't women think of anything else?

"What are you glaring at?"

Mike jerked and looked up. Callie stood there, fresh and smiling in her yellow sundress. He'd been so deep in thought, he hadn't heard her drive up the hill. "Don't you ever wear a jacket?" he demanded.

She shrugged. "I don't get cold—just hot-blooded, I guess."

"Very funny."

"I'm glad you're amused."

"I'm not, thank you very much."

"Sheesh, what a grump. Your sense of humor sure needs some work." Callie lifted the hair from her neck and combed her fingers through its silky length.

Mike's gaze followed each nuance of the innately feminine gesture.

"Sorry. I...still have a headache," he found himself saying. A pure fabrication, but easier than explaining his confused feelings. "From last night. I didn't mean to be difficult."

"That's all right." She shrugged her bare shoulders, exposed around thin ribbon straps. "There's no need to fuss about me—I have a high tolerance for the cold. And besides, it isn't really cold up here, not right now."

"It is during the winter."

"But I won't be here in the winter." She smiled again and turned toward the house.

Mike felt curiously bereft when she walked away. Callie was a nice kid and he'd been an impossible grump since she'd arrived. No wonder she was intent on getting his goat.

As for the magazine? He shouldn't have been so surprised she'd teased him—Elaine would have gotten great fun out of it, too. He didn't doubt that his sister saw him as a big doofus, a little dumb and comical, with all the grace and tact of a Mack truck. Callie probably felt the same way, lumping him into the same category with her own brothers.

Somehow the realization didn't comfort him quite as much as he'd expected, and Mike frowned as he followed her into the house. He found her in the kitchen, which cheered him up immensely.

"How did everything go...down at the office?" he asked, determined to show he was over his embarrassment.

"Okay. By the way, is that computer for company use, or just cargo en route?"

"It's ours," Mike said gloomily. "But it doesn't work right. The screen keeps going blank, and there's all these little pictures that don't make any sense when the darn thing *is* working."

Screen saver, Callie thought. And the "pictures" were part of the programming. Mike and his partners were out of touch with the modern world—how could three such intelligent men be so helpless?

"I'll see what I can do with it," she said, instead of explaining. It wouldn't hurt to look like a miracle worker, saving an expensive investment and putting it to use.

"You know how to work a computer?" Mike asked, surprise in his voice.

"Of course I do." Scowling, Callie thrust her hand in the grocery bag she brought in from the truck. Her fingers closed over a banana. If she lobbed it right she could hit Mike square between the eyes.

"Why don't I take you out to dinner?" he asked.

She paused. This was promising; maybe she shouldn't throw the banana after all.

"So you don't have to cook," he continued. "I know you had a hard day, and I'll bet your ankle is sore."

Still hidden from sight, her fingernails cut into the banana peel. He'd done it again, consigned her to that comfortable category of nice-girl-who-cooks. It went right along with the nice-preacher's-daughter-who's-just-like-a-sister routine. Well, she *did* cook, but Mike wouldn't be tasting her cooking anytime soon!

"Don't worry about me," Callie said. "I won't be a nuisance using the kitchen while I'm here." She dropped the mutilated piece of fruit and took a carton of yogurt from the sack. "I just need a little space in the refrigerator, that's all."

Dismay registered on his face. "No...that is, I don't mind if you use the kitchen."

"No." She shook her head vigorously. "You're polite to offer, but I have no intention of getting in your way. To tell the truth, I prefer to just eat fruit and yogurt and stuff. Cooking is such a bother and I want to spend my free time enjoying Alaska. I won't be here that long."

Mike's visions of caramel pecan pancakes crumbled. And the prospects for hot coffee waiting in the morning looked pretty dim, too.

"And I'm having dinner with Ross tonight, anyway," she added.

"Oh."

Not only was he not going to eat pancakes, but he'd spend the evening wondering if Ross was any more of a gentleman than Donovan. Funny, he'd never questioned their morals before. They were friends who respected each other's space. *Keep it legal* was the most they'd ever advised when it came to women and recreation.

"Uh...Callie," Mike said at last. "Ross isn't the marrying kind, any more than Donovan. I'd hate for you to get the wrong idea, thinking they had...er..."

"Honorable intentions?" Callie grinned. "Mike, you're so old-fashioned. It's sweet that you're so protective, but I'm all grown up."

"Of course, but you've been sheltered all your life and don't know what guys can be like...up...here." He faltered. "That is...it can get lonely."

"I certainly hope so," she returned cheerfully.

Hellfire. The headache he'd fabricated was coming

back for real. He was being punished for every prank, every peccadillo and sin he'd ever committed. "Callie—"

She interrupted him with a laugh. "Lighten up, Mike. I've known the facts of life for a long time. As for being sheltered, preacher's kids see everything that happens—good and bad—same as anyone else. Only, we see more of what happens, because when trouble visits a family in the church, it also visits the preacher."

He hadn't thought of that. Funny, there were a lot of things he hadn't considered when it came to Callie. She was part of his childhood—the part he took for granted. Sort of like his mother's apple butter or the rain in Washington.

Callie was the sweet-faced brat who'd giggled at his sister's slumber parties, and quietly worked for hours in the church kitchen following his grandfather's funeral. She was what then? Thirteen? Even at that age the women had asked her opinion and treated her like an adult. *Expected* her to be an adult.

Strange... Had Callie ever gotten to be a child? *Really* a child? Not just giggling at rare sleepovers, but living in that happy, joyful state where play was more important than responsibility?

He didn't know. When it came right down to it, he didn't know much about Callie at all. Mike looked at her, once again seeing a stranger instead of the girl he's always known.

"What's the matter?" Callie asked as she folded her grocery bag and stored it neatly under the sink. "Do I have motor grease on my face? I'm not surprised—I still can't believe the difference between this house and that office. You must be schizophrenic."

"No...but I'm glad you like the house."

"It's great," she said, enthused. "It's so spacious and comfortable, with all those porches and wide windows."

Mike cleared his throat, still trying to make sense of the jumbled thoughts inside his mind, and annoyed that his first thought was *yeah, great...but you don't have to heat this place in the winter.*

Why should Callie understand the practicalities of an Alaskan winter? He'd bought the house without understanding it himself—and the following summer had spent more than the purchase price in modernizing and insulating the place. As a result, heating wasn't nearly the problem it used to be.

"It was originally built as a fishing lodge," he explained. "There used to be a number of cabins out back...for clients."

"I see." A thoughtful expression filled her eyes. "Are you planning to use it as commercial property again? It's a little big for one person."

Mike grimaced. He'd told himself the house was an investment—if he got tired of the air-transit business, he could turn to running a fishing lodge. Only...he'd never get tired of flying, and the lodge was never a commercial success, even in its heyday. He just plain liked living here. A man could spread out and feel comfortable in a house like this.

"Nope, it's just me and the bears," he said.

"Oh." Callie looked at her watch. "You know, I'd better get ready before Ross gets here. I don't want to keep him waiting."

"Uh...Callie?"

She paused, and Mike stood there, tongued-tied all at once. In her pale yellow sundress she looked like an exotic butterfly, brightening the age-darkened walls of the kitchen. And when he reached out to cup her cheek in his hand, her eyes widened.

"Mike?"

Her light floral fragrance washed over him, stirring a memory, deep in the back of his mind. Maybe she'd been wearing that same scent when she'd fallen over him the night before. He'd been trying to remember what happened after Callie got back from her date with Donovan—even one blackout night was enough to make him uncomfortable.

And he'd had that dream again…a dream inter-mixed with a long-ago memory of a sexy kiss.

Jeez. You'd think a man would achieve some ma-turity when he reached a certain age. He'd stop fan-tasizing about a hot kiss, sweet laughter and curious fingers roaming over his body. After all, a relationship was more than hot sex, and Mike didn't even want a relationship.

"What is it, Mike?"

"Please be careful," he said. Wow, her skin was so soft, dewy silk against his rough calluses. "I don't want you getting hurt."

Her eyelashes swept down, forming dark crescents against a creamy background. "Because I'm just like a sister, right?"

Sister? No, Callie wasn't anything like his sister. While Mike wasn't exactly clear about his feelings for her, he knew they weren't brotherly. He wasn't con-fused about his sister, and at the moment Callie was making him feel damned confused.

"Let's just say I care about you. Okay?"

She looked at him for a long while, then smiled faintly. "Okay."

Chapter Four

Let's just say that I care about you.

Callie paused while brushing her hair. Hardly a declaration of undying love, but better than nothing...and enough to keep her from throwing something out of pure exasperation.

She had to keep chipping away at Mike's defenses, make him see her as a woman. It was a twofold problem, because she also wanted him to marry her, and Michael Fitzpatrick's views on marriage had always been quite clear.

Fine for other guys if they get caught, but give him a life of freedom.

"Men." Callie scowled. At heart she didn't think any man truly grew up. They stayed little boys, sneaking their fingers into the cookie jar, and acting all innocent when they got caught. Of course, that was part of their charm.

Her scowl faded and she shrugged philosophically. Elaine always said a man chased a woman until she caught him. But Callie intended to chase Mike until *he* caught *her*. The trick was not letting him know she was chasing him.

Anyway, she wasn't finished with Donovan and Ross—they were fun, gallantly admiring and made her feel pampered. *They* didn't have a problem with her clothing, and they had made it clear they'd be more than happy to console her if she changed her mind about Mike.

Callie dropped the hairbrush onto the dresser. Changing her mind was a distinct possibility if Mike didn't straighten out. She didn't plan on spending her life being the ''nice'' preacher's daughter. It wasn't just about sex, it was about being a partner, an equal—knowing your husband will share his problems and let you worry with him.

And it was also about sex.

Hmm.

She stalked to the closet and took out her dress for the evening. Mike was worried about her getting cold? This should show him—her arms and shoulders would be completely covered. Callie held the soft jersey knit against her, noting the way it draped and clung to her body. She smiled and tossed the dress to the bed. Perfect.

Shrugging out of the yellow sundress, Callie changed into lacy, French-cut underwear. She looked at her reflection critically, trying to decide if she should wear a bra. Maybe she wasn't the most gorgeous woman in the world, but she had her good points. Grinning, she decided a bra wasn't necessary. The unfettered look had turned Mike into a raving idiot the night before, maybe it would do the same tonight.

It was the first step in her plan—make Mike see her as a desirable woman. That had to come first, because he'd never fall in love with a woman he considered a "nice kid."

Mike sipped a cup of coffee and focused on the stack of paperwork on the table, yet all he could think about was Callie taking a shower and getting dressed for her "date." He couldn't quite visualize her naked, which was the only thing keeping him rational at the moment.

It was crazy.

He should be pleased with the way things had turned out. Callie was making very little impact on his life. She didn't expect to be fed or entertained, and she was so quiet, he hardly knew she was in the house.

Yup, things were working out better than he'd thought when she'd arrived in Alaska instead of Elaine. Just fine. Perfect, in fact.

His hand bumped the cup, splattering coffee across the table. Mike swore quietly; he shouldn't be drinking caffeine so late in the day, it made him jittery.

Oh, really?

And Callie has nothing to do with it?

Mike's conscience jeered and he sighed. Okay, he was jittery from wondering what Callie would do next. Not that it was any of his business—she'd been perfectly clear about that, but heart attacks weren't fun. And she'd nearly given him a heart attack with her skimpy little outfits.

"Hey, pal." Ross knocked on the back door and stuck his head inside. "Is Callie ready?"

Mike glared. "How should I know?"

His friend shrugged, unperturbed. "We were lucky

she could come up here for the summer. Not that I have anything against Elaine, but Callie is something else, isn't she?''

Something else... Yeah, Callie was a whole lot of something, Mike just didn't know what. ''I thought you swore off women,'' he muttered. ''The marrying kind, that is.''

''I did, but Callie's in a class by herself.'' Ross took a cola from the refrigerator with the casual ease of an old friend. He popped the top and took a long swallow. ''She's already fixed that mess with old man Pinsky, and mailed outstanding bills for the past two months,'' he enthused. ''And you should listen to her on the phone—she could charm grizzlies out of their dens. She'll be great for business.''

''That's nice.'' Mike stabbed the signature line of a check with his pen. Hearing how wonderfully Callie was doing at the office should have made him happy— it was the whole reason she was in Alaska. Yet he was dismally aware she'd already crept into every part of his life *and* his thoughts.

''It's a little early to know for certain, but we might want her to stay on permanently,'' Ross murmured. ''You know Delia doesn't want to come back.''

The check tore as Mike yanked it from the pad, and he crumpled it into a ball. ''Callie is here on a lark,'' he growled, tossing the wadded paper in the waste-basket. ''She doesn't have any idea of what winters are like in Alaska, or how isolated it can be. She'd go out of her mind in a month.''

Ross crushed his now-empty soda can and stored it in the recycle container near the door. ''Nonsense. Callie's a grown woman, and she'd make some guy a great wife.''

Mike frowned. "You aren't serious, are you? You just met Callie. That's hardly enough time to start thinking about the big *M*. Besides, I thought you said women were just out for a free meal ticket."

"Callie's different. Anyway, I'm not planning on proposing tonight, if that's what you're asking." Ross looked up, eyes widening, and whistled. "But all things being equal, I might change my mind."

Instantly Mike turned his head and saw Callie walking through the door. For a moment, he didn't understand what Ross was talking about, then the air whooshed from his lungs.

The dress should have been demure—it covered her from midcalf to her throat. *That's* where demure ended. Made of some kind of clingy stuff, the deep blue-green fabric draped every curve of her body like a second skin. Somehow it was even more provocative than the black dress she'd worn on her date with Donovan, because it challenged a guy to think of creative ways to get it off....

"That..." He cleared his throat. "Callie, I don't think you shou—"

"Don't bother thinking," Ross interrupted. "You're a knockout, Miss Webster."

She laughed. "Thanks. I was afraid I'd be overdressed for the restaurant, but Mike's been worried I'll catch cold, so I decided to wear this instead of something else. See, Mike? I'm all covered—arms, shoulders and legs. I'm quite dowdy."

Callie whirled and Mike gulped. Who'd have imagined that wholesome Callie could turn into a Delilah? And if she thought that dress was dowdy, he'd eat his boots.

"Cal—"

"I'll see you tomorrow, Mike," she said, patting his cheek. The wicked amusement in her green eyes made him grit his teeth. *Miss Webster* had gotten herself a devious...and thoroughly intriguing sense of humor. "Don't wait up."

"Don't wait...?" He gritted his teeth. "I happened to fall asleep on the couch, that's all. I didn't wait up for you last night."

A patient look spread across Callie's face. "I know you didn't, Mike. It's just an expression." She glanced at Ross and shrugged. "Does he always have so much trouble understanding...everything?"

There seemed to be a double message in the question, yet Mike couldn't figure out what it might be—and that made him even more nervous. Callie was up to something and he didn't have the slightest notion what to do about it.

His friend ducked his head and cleared his throat. "I'd say Mike is just as befuddled as the rest of us."

"Us? You mean men, don't you?" she asked with a shade of tartness in her voice.

"Yeah, right." Ross grinned. "Though I'm being disloyal to my sex to agree."

Callie laughed and tucked her arm into his. "Never mind. A little disloyalty can be good for you. Besides, I appreciate open-minded men."

Mike slumped deeper into his chair and gazed at the stack of paperwork in front of him. A little gremlin inside his head kept saying this wasn't really Callie, but a long-lost twin, raised by gypsies. Except Callie didn't have a long-lost twin, raised by gypsies or not. She didn't even have a sister—just two brothers who obviously didn't give a rat's behind what happened to their innocent young sister.

Because if they did, they would never have let her come to Alaska with a suitcase full of clothing designed to raise a man's blood pressure.

"See you tomorrow, Mike," Callie called as she and Ross walked out the back door.

"Mmm," he mumbled in acknowledgment.

See you tomorrow?

Exactly how long did it take to eat dinner and come home? Kachelak wasn't a bustling metropolis; they had two restaurants, a little hamburger stand and a pizza joint that doubled as an accountant's office during tax season. It wasn't the kind of place you spent hours lingering over a twelve-course gourmet meal.

Mike rubbed his newly aching temples. He needed a good night's sleep, that's all. Sleep that wasn't disturbed by Scotch or sensual dreams, or the discomfort of sleeping on a couch. And he didn't need to worry about Callie.... As Ross said, she was a grown woman capable of taking care of herself.

Right?

Yeah, right.

Just because she looked like sex incarnate didn't mean anything. She was still Preacher Webster's daughter, a nice girl despite what she said. It didn't seem right having any heated feelings for Callie, especially under the circumstances. She was living in his house, under his protection.

Rubbing the back of his neck, Mike stared at the ceiling. The same natural log beams that adorned the rest of the house were darker in here. A woman would prefer a different kind of ceiling—clean and bright, with Sheetrock covering the logs. Callie would probably like it painted a pale yellow or green...something crisp and light to brighten the winter.

A cold sweat broke out on Mike's forehead and he groaned.

Callie?

Callie wasn't spending the winter in Alaska, and he wasn't going to remodel his house to make her happy. At the end of the summer he'd put her on a plane back to Washington and forget this whole uncomfortable mess.

Still…he glanced around, trying to see the place through a woman's eyes. Since he didn't cook himself, he'd neglected it when he modernized the house. He ought to renovate the kitchen to equal the rest of the house. If nothing else, he'd be able to sell it easier if he ever decided to move. And pale yellow would look real nice in here, especially during the long winter.

Right.

It was a business decision…and didn't have anything to do with Callie.

Callie took a bite of her dessert and smiled at Ross McCoy sitting across the table. He was an awfully nice guy, and he'd been doing his best to make her welcome in Alaska, unlike Mike, who still seemed anxious to stick her on the next plane out of the state.

At the thought of Mike, Callie's good humor faltered. Would he ever come around, or would she die an old lady still trying to make him notice her legs?

"Tell me something, why are you and Donovan helping me with Mike?" she asked. "I thought dedicated bachelors always stuck together."

Ross's eyes twinkled. "You're perfect for him, that's why. Besides, watching him dangle for the summer is going to be the most entertainment we've had in a long time."

She wrinkled her nose. "I hope it won't take all summer."

"It won't, but if worse comes to worst, you can stay for the winter. You're great in the office—decorative and useful at the same time."

Callie threw her napkin at him. "That's a chauvinistic attitude."

He shrugged. "It comes with the territory—this isn't the most liberated state in the country."

"Hmm." She concentrated on her cup of coffee and thought about Ross's oblique warning. It was something to think about. She liked what she'd seen of Alaska, but it wasn't Washington. There would be a lot of changes to make if she ended up living here.

If?

Callie gulped. No matter how hard she tried to be positive, doubts crept in; even now she was a little surprised by her boldness in coming to Alaska. It had been a spur-of-the-moment decision, but with her biological clock ticking, and the emptiness of another summer stretching before her, she'd grabbed the chance.

Summers were the worst.

Her friends were always busy doing things with their families, taking advantage of the school vacation. They tried to include her, but it didn't replace having a family of her own. She'd considered alternatives like adoption, but what she really wanted was Mike as her husband, and Mike's baby...growing inside of her.

She'd even been tempted to swallow her pride and beg Mike to just get her pregnant—nothing else, no commitments or promises. It wouldn't be a perfect solution, but at least she'd have *part* of what she wanted.

"Are you all right, Callie? You look unhappy."

Startled, she looked at Ross. "No…not really. I was just thinking."

"About Mike?"

"Who else?" She traced a pattern on the tablecloth with her fingernail. "He's changed a lot over the years. I wonder… What makes you think Mike and I are so right for each other?"

Ross smiled kindly. "Instinct. Did you know he's got pictures of you? Ones with Elaine. I asked once, and he said you were a great kid. He had this silly, affectionate expression, so it was obvious he cared."

"Kid?" Callie said, pleased and annoyed at the same time. "That's just like him—he refuses to see I'm a grown woman."

"Oh…" Ross shook his head and laughed. "I wouldn't worry about that. I know Mike. His mind might say you're a kid, but his body disagrees. *Bigtime.* After a few more days he's going to be frothing at the mouth."

A bubble of delight grew inside of Callie—Mike frothing at the mouth was a pleasing notion. After all, there were lots of ways to make him better, and they all involved some very cozy snuggling.

"And, Callie?"

She looked at Ross, seeing his face turn serious. "Yes?"

"Even if things don't work out, you can still stay. Alaska needs women like you, and I happen to think you're pretty special myself."

The unexpected warmth in his gaze made her flush.

She'd found a surprising set of allies in Mike's partners, and she lay in bed that night, thinking about what Ross had told her, but mostly thinking about Mike.

The emotion growing in her heart had nothing to do

with a silly girlhood crush. And while Mike might not be in love, it was encouraging to know he hadn't forgotten her over the years.

Ten days later Callie glanced at her watch, then hurriedly shoved a client's billing record into a file cabinet. It was just after 7:00 a.m., but Ross McCoy had a cargo run scheduled to the Arctic Circle and he'd asked her to go with him. They would sleep over and fly back on Sunday.

Callie grinned when she thought of Mike's reaction to her little expedition—as though she planned to parachute nude into New York's Times Square.

Absolutely not. You aren't going anywhere. What would your father say?

He'd say have a good time, and don't get eaten by a polar bear. Fathers worry a lot about hungry polar bears—it's a dad thing.

Very funny.

Mike had glared fiercely and stomped away, only to return an hour later and start the argument all over again. For someone who'd gone into business with Ross and Donovan, he sure didn't trust the two men. Of course, she hadn't bothered to explain they'd arranged for two separate motel rooms...especially since he should have realized that fact on his own.

Mike was developing an awfully short fuse, and Callie's grin faded as she remembered the absurd argument he'd started with Donovan the day before. She didn't want to cause problems between the three partners. Donovan and Ross kept saying not to worry, that everything would be fine once Mike took his head out of the sand and figured things out.

Maybe...but it didn't make her feel good.

She'd always been a peacemaker, so being the source of conflict was an uncomfortable switch. She sighed and scanned another client's records.

"Callie?"

Mike.

She made a face and sighed. Loving Mike and dealing with him were two entirely different things. Did he hope to ruin the plans she'd made with Ross? For that matter, where *was* Ross? They should have left an hour ago.

"Yes?"

He stood at the door, rough and sexy at the same time, and her stomach did a cartwheel. Dressed in a black shirt and jeans, with a dark beard shadow on his face, Mike did things to her that no man had ever been able to do. And it was a real shame. Both Donovan and Ross were terrific guys, but she had to get stuck on a man who saw her as a cross between Shirley Temple and the Flying Nun.

"Uh…" Mike rubbed his chin, seeming oddly uncomfortable. "Ross called after you left the house— he's got a migraine and can't fly today."

"I see." Callie's eyes narrowed. If Ross really had a migraine, then he had her sympathy; if *Mike* had anything to do with the change in her plans she'd serve him up for dinner. Thank goodness she had a contingency plan up her sleeve.

"Er…he said to apologize."

She closed the drawer of the file cabinet and shrugged her shoulders. "That's all right, I'm just sorry he's sick. I'll give Donovan a call and tell him we can go to the Kenai Wildlife Refuge, after all. He invited me after I accepted Ross's invitation, and he was really disappointed when I had to say 'no.' Maybe we could camp down there overnight—he said he has a lot of outdoor gear."

"No!" Mike practically lunged forward and snatched the receiver from her hand. He plunked it back onto the cradle with a resounding smack. "That is...I thought I'd take you myself."

"You don't have time for hiking, remember?"

A muscle ticked in Mike's jaw and Callie bit her lip to keep from laughing. She wasn't being very nice, but vamps couldn't be nice to get what they wanted.

"Not to Kenai," he said, visibly gathering his patience. "We'll fly to the Arctic Circle, just like you planned."

"Oh?" Callie murmured, trying to sound casually disinterested...yet her heart kicked into overdrive and she barely kept from shouting a resounding *yes*.

"Yeah. You've been doing a ton of work here— you didn't even take last weekend off. Hell, we're even making more money. You deserve a sightseeing trip, and I'd really like to take you myself."

Mike wanted to take her sightseeing.

The cautious part of Callie's nature told her not to get her hopes up, while the naturally buoyant part was dancing a jig through her tummy. Of course, that part had been dancing a jig ever since she'd arrived and seen Mike's reaction to her red tube top. A man couldn't be that upset about her exposing a little skin without being the tiniest bit interested, could he?

"I don't know..." she murmured, trying to sound reluctant. "It seems rude not to call Donovan. He did ask first."

"Forget Donovan."

He sounded so disgruntled, her spirits rose even higher. In the beginning, she'd made dates with

Mike's partners to keep him from guessing her real reason for being in Alaska, not to make him jealous. She'd reasoned he couldn't think she was out to catch *him* if she was dating someone else. But even if she hadn't done it to make him jealous, those dates had helped him see her in a new way...as a woman.

At least...she thought he was starting to see her as a woman; with Mike it was hard to tell.

"Er...aren't you busy?" she asked.

"Nope." All at once a boyish grin curved his mouth. "Come on, it'll be fun, Callie. We've never really done anything together, not even when we were kids. To be honest..." He stopped and looked perplexed. "We don't know each other that well. We should get better acquainted."

Hallelujah, Callie cheered silently. Maybe he'd stop dismissing her as the sweet-but-annoying-kid-sister type. "At least you know I won't steal the silver," she teased.

"True."

To her amazement, Mike reached out and brushed errant strands of hair from her forehead. The hard calluses on his fingers caught the strands like magnets, pulling more to join them until he was completely entangled, and he finally gave her a helpless expression.

He was so close, Callie could smell the warm, masculine scent of him, and a piercing ache went through her body. She'd like to cuddle...feel welcome to slide into his arms and put her head on his chest. Instead, she lifted her hand and freed his fingers, shivering with sensations both hot and cold.

"Sorry," he murmured.

"Th-that's okay." Callie nervously cleared her

throat. Her breasts had instinctively tightened from his warmth and touch, and she prayed he wouldn't notice.

"I packed an overnight bag," Mike said, his voice low and rough. "Ross said he made reservations in Barrow."

"It's too far for a one-day trip."

"Yeah."

Mike winced at his moronic brain and hurriedly stepped back. Callie probably thought he'd been making a pass at her, and he wasn't entirely sure himself. It was hard having his perceptions slammed this way. Why couldn't she have stayed the nice preacher's kid? That *Callie* wouldn't have been making feel so confused about everything, and she would have fixed him coffee and caramel pecan pancakes in the morning.

He coughed to clear his throat and hoped she wouldn't look in the general direction of his jeans. It had been at least fifteen years since he'd blushed, but he'd probably turn brick-red if Callie Webster realized he was having an involuntary reaction to touching her.

"I...uh, I'll go do a preflight check on Piper," he said, turning quickly.

"But Ross was supposed to take a load to Kotzebue. We planned to take one of the smaller planes to Anchorage and pick up the cargo plane from there," she protested, stopping him at the door.

Mike looked over his shoulder. "That's been changed. I called Travis Black to take the load. He's already on his way."

"Oh." Callie blinked, and she took a clipboard from the desk, scanning it quickly. "But I'm sure it's Travis's weekend off."

As he turned around, Mike snatched his coat from the rack and dangled it over his arm, covering a stra-

tegic location on his body. "Travis never objects to
extra flight time, and this way you'll have more time
to see Point Barrow," he explained. "Anyway, aerial
tours are a lot easier in a Piper Comanche—a cargo
plane isn't practical for that kind of thing."

"I suppose. Are you sure it isn't any trouble?"

Mike groaned silently. Of course it was a lot of
trouble. He didn't mind, and neither did Travis Black,
but rearranging flight schedules and using multiple
planes was a lot of trouble...just like Callie. She'd
been trouble from the minute she had arrived in
Alaska.

On the other hand, this was an opportunity to talk
some sense into the woman. They'd be on the plane
for several hours, calmly discussing this, that and everything. Sooner or later he'd be able to impress on
her that Ross and Donovan were great guys, just not
the type of determined bachelor she should be dating.

Actually, he wasn't too comfortable with the
thought of Callie dating anyone, but that emotion
didn't bear close examination.

"Mike?" Callie prodded.

"Uh...not to worry," he said cheerfully. "I've got
it all covered. Besides, we both deserve a relaxing
weekend."

She gave him a small, enigmatic smile that made
him uncomfortable all over again. "All right," she
agreed. "If you insist."

Chapter Five

"To the north...see? That's the Tanana River," Mike said, pointing to a ribbon of silver, winding through the land far below. He dipped the wing to give Callie a better view. "And Nenana is off that way."

"That's where they hold the Ice Classic, the lottery you won?"

"Yup. It would have taken a lot longer to start the Triple M if we hadn't bet on the breakup time of the ice. Our savings and the stake we got from the lottery pool, plus the loan from old man Jackson, was enough to buy our first cargo plane."

Mike brought the Piper level again and glanced at Callie from the corner of his eye. She seemed happy and relaxed, so it might be the right moment to mention that Donovan and Ross weren't her type.

Casually.

She'd been completely unreasonable every other time he'd tried to discuss the matter, but things were different now. After all, they were having a nice time, enjoying each other's company. What could be more natural? Mike cleared his throat and fiddled with the controls of the plane.

"You've certainly been busy since getting here," he said, pretending to concentrate on a distant point of the landscape, far below them.

"I'm having a great time," Callie agreed.

She smiled and Mike's stomach did a curious loop-the-loop that was totally out of character for him. He'd never gone wild over a woman—no outrageous teen-age crushes or soul-searching adult love affairs, just good times. The women he dated wanted the same thing he did—uncomplicated, no-one-gets-hurt type of relationships. So how could Callie make him feel like a callow adolescent after all these years? It didn't make sense.

He gazed out the cockpit window; his feelings for Callie Webster were all mixed up. In less than two weeks she'd moved into his house, gotten involved in every aspect of his business and looked so sexy, his tongue was practically hanging out of his mouth. If he wasn't careful, he'd develop a permanent drool.

Don't think about it.

Good advice. He was supposed to be warning Callie *away* from the dedicated bachelor types that abounded in Alaska, not thinking about…well…undressing her himself. She wouldn't be any better off with him, than one of his partners.

He cleared his throat again. "That new schedule you set up is terrific, and you've gotten folks to pay bills we never expected to see a dime from."

She twisted in her seat, reminding him painfully of her slim hips and nicely rounded bustline. "Pretty good for a preacher's kid, huh? I guess my experience volunteering at the church is a little more valuable than you thought," she murmured.

"Aw, Callie," Mike protested. "You aren't going to bring that up all summer, are you? I admit I was wrong."

Wrong, Callie mused wryly. Wrong about a lot of things, if you asked her.

"To be honest, I'm also a private management consultant," she said, deciding to tell him the truth. "I've worked with a lot of different companies. No airlines, but everything from restaurants to major firms in Seattle."

"You're kidding."

"Nope...I've got my own office—Callie's Concepts."

"I see." A small frown creased the space between Mike's eyes, and he was silent as he absorbed this new chunk of information. A peculiar range of emotions crossed his face, and after several minutes he shook his head. "Uh...it must have been hard to leave for several months."

"Not really—I needed a vacation. And I've got a great assistant running the place."

"This isn't exactly a vacation," Mike felt compelled to point out, his brain reeling.

Callie was a management consultant? She had her own business? Since when? Elaine talked about Callie occasionally, but she'd never mentioned any of this. It didn't fit with his image of her—the small-town preacher's kid who still played the organ in her father's church. But then, a lot of things didn't fit about Callie anymore.

"Don't worry about me. I know exactly what I'm doing."

Did she? Mike rubbed the back of his neck, trying to ease the tension in his muscles. Every time he had Callie figured out, she went and proved him wrong. And he still hadn't found a way of bringing Ross and Donovan into the discussion.

"Uh, I'm sorry Ross couldn't take you today."

She snorted gently. "No, you're not."

His gaze narrowed. Of course, Callie was right, he didn't like the idea of his partners coming near her. And his reasons were getting more muddled by the minute. For a brief, wishful moment Mike thought about the good old days—before Callie had arrived and turned him into an irrational, drooling idiot with his brains in his pants.

"Callie, I just don't want—"

"Please, no more lectures about being careful around your friends, and not getting the wrong idea about them," she snapped. "Huh, and I honestly thought you wanted to spend the weekend together without any ulterior motives. I should have called Donovan and gone to Kenai with him."

Mike groaned. He hadn't said a word about being careful, or any of the things he'd planned to say, so Callie must have read his mind. She had a habit of doing that lately, and it was damned embarrassing if she realized he'd fantasized—more than once—about making love to her.

He squirmed a moment, trying to banish the thought from his head. Callie couldn't really read his mind, so she couldn't know about his inappropriate feelings.

The crackle of the radio distracted him and he talked back and forth with the air-traffic controller in Fairbanks. Although the Piper Comanche could make it to Point Barrow without refueling, he preferred to enter the Arctic Circle with full tanks. Better to be safe than sorry.

"We'll set down in Fairbanks and refuel," he explained at Callie's questioning look.

Callie didn't mind. She was still annoyed with Mike, but she hadn't expected her manhunting project to be easy, and the trip wasn't over yet. As long as they were together, that's all that mattered. They didn't even have to go to Barrow—she'd have plenty of time to see polar bears...after they were married.

"Will it take long?" Callie asked as they descended.

"Not too long. They're fast. Lots of small planes going in and out. Alaska is the 'flyingist' state in the union—at least that's what we claim."

"Okay."

As Mike had predicted, they were in and out of the Fairbanks airport in nothing flat, and she settled back into her seat for the second leg of their trip. The mountains were coming closer and closer when she noticed Mike frowning.

"Is something wrong?"

"It's probably nothing." He tapped the instrument panel and frowned again. "There's a temperature gauge overheating."

She took a quick breath. "Is it serious?"

His frown turned into a reassuring smile. "No, but I'll have to set down again to check the engine. It isn't worth taking any chances. Besides, it's a flight regulation."

Callie watched Mike's quiet competence as he handled the controls and she tried not to worry. He was a great pilot—according to Donovan, he could fly through a hurricane and come out in one piece.

"We're all right, Callie," Mike murmured. He eased the plane to lower altitude.

"I know."

"Sure, but you'll lose the feeling in your hands if you don't unclench your fists." He briefly covered her clenched fingers and squeezed.

"Oh." Callie glanced at her white knuckles and laughed self-consciously. "I trust you...I really do."

"It's okay—you're not used to flying," he said gently. "I promise, this is just a precaution. We'll be heading over the Brooks Mountain Range pretty soon and I wouldn't want to have trouble there. It's not the most hospitable landscape in the world, even in the summertime."

"Of course."

Mike's smile turned to gentle teasing. "Think about it, Callie. I'm a Fitzpatrick—I've got Irish luck and charm protecting me."

She giggled, more from nerves than humor. "Charm doesn't protect you."

"Well, it must be good for something."

Good for seducing women, Callie thought ruefully. His teasing helped ease her tension, yet she couldn't help a silent prayer of relief when the Comanche swept smoothly into the tiny airstrip.

A truly ancient man appeared from a sturdy building at the edge of the field. He drifted toward the plane at a leisurely pace and stood for several minutes gazing at them while Mike shut down the engine and opened the door of the plane.

"Trouble?" the old man asked finally, taking a toothpick from his mouth. His weathered face showed the signs of long, hard years.

"It won't take long—I just want to check the engine," Mike explained. "A temp gauge is acting up."

The man nodded and turned around again. With the same slow pace he headed back to the structure and disappeared inside, the sum total of his conversation being a single word.

Callie stole a glance at Mike, her lips twitching. "Is he one of the lonely bachelors you keep telling me about? The type I should watch out for? I'll sure have to move quick to keep from being caught by him."

Mike scowled. "That's Curdgeon Post. He's an old sourdough who refuses to go to the pioneer home in Fairbanks. Curdgeon's a stubborn old goat—he spent fifty years trying to find gold in the Yukon and ended up here."

"Alone?"

"Yeah, alone."

Callie looked at the solitary building and shivered. They were inside the Arctic Circle, and she couldn't imagine spending the winter in such a place. "Maybe he was looking for the wrong thing."

"What should he have looked for?"

Love, was her silent answer, but she shrugged, certain Mike wasn't ready to accept the importance of love in any man's life. He knew what she meant, anyway. His shrewd gaze hadn't left her face, and he wasn't stupid.

After a long moment of silence Mike climbed out of the plane and Callie followed, happy to stretch her legs again. The windswept airstrip lay near the base of the mountains, which rose to the north. It was beautiful, in a stark kind of way. Tundra spreading out in an unwavering sea of greens and grays, and the gray-white of the distant mountain peaks.

"I'm going to take a walk," Callie murmured.

Mike's answer was a mumbled grunt from the bowels of the engine, along with a "Don't get lost."

She rolled her eyes. Where would she go? There weren't any towns, hiking trails, or historical monuments in sight...just a lonely building, with an even lonelier man sitting inside it.

At the door of the small building, she took a deep breath and knocked. After a full minute the door opened and Curdgeon Post glared out at her.

"Go away," he growled.

She scuffed the ground with her foot, then gestured around the barren landscape. "There's nowhere to go. Do you mind if I come in while Mike is checking the engine?"

He blinked, seeming astonished. "Why?"

Callie swallowed. Maybe this hadn't been such a good idea, but Curdgeon reminded her of a man she knew back home—his family gone, with no one to care about him. It was terrible for anyone to feel like that. So she gathered her courage, smiled and opened her mouth.

"I just wanted to visit, Mr. Post. I'll bet you know a lot about Alaska, and some great stories."

"You ain't from the north?"

She cast a quick look at Mike working on the plane and shrugged. "Not yet."

"Humph. Don't have no time. Go away."

He started to close the door and Callie determinedly put a hand out to stop him. "I'm sorry, we haven't been introduced. My name is Calliope Webster, but everyone calls me Callie."

The old man's lips shifted beneath his white beard. "Calliope?"

"I know. Isn't it awful?"

"T'aint so bad." He grasped her fingers with sudden enthusiasm and pumped her arm. "I never met no one called Calliope."

"And I've never met anyone called Curdgeon."

"Er..." He put a finger to his lips and looked around with furtive care, as though fearful someone would hear him. "It's really Enoch," he whispered.

It wasn't a strange name, but it sounded strange coming from the crusty fellow. Sort of like hearing the queen of England say her name was Liz. "Oh...why does everyone call you Curdgeon?"

"I been called that fer fifty years. They'd say, 'You're a mean ole curdgeon, Post.' An' pretty soon it was just Curdgeon."

Callie bit her lip to keep from grinning. *Curmudgeon.* Enoch Post had been called a curmudgeon so often, everyone thought it was really his name. And it wasn't funny, not really. Beneath his tough exterior was a nice person...just a little rough around the edges.

"Well, I'd like to call you Enoch, if you don't mind."

"Guess it'd be all right—if'n ya don't tell no one. I got a pot of coffee on the stove, Calliope. Want a cup?"

She nodded and followed him inside. "I'd love some."

Mike patiently checked the last gauge and made some final adjustments. He hadn't found anything wrong with the engine, but he wanted to be certain everything was safe before he took Callie up in the air again. For reasons he didn't want to explore, it seemed more important than normal to be safe with her...and the Triple M already had a stellar reputation for safety.

He'd expected Callie to hang around asking questions, yet he hadn't seen her for at least twenty minutes. Straightening, Mike looked around the bleak airfield.

No Callie.

He frowned and covered the engine.

Since Curdgeon Post had raised inhospitality to an art form, it wasn't likely she was with him. Mike walked around the plane, checking in every direction.

"That's odd," he muttered to himself, even peering inside the Comanche cargo space to be sure Callie hadn't climbed back inside without his noticing. The only place she could have gone was to visit Curdgeon...which boggled the mind. Curdgeon had a reputation for unfriendliness that rivaled a lean, mean bear waking from hibernation.

He wasn't a bad guy, just set in his ways. Years before, he'd offered Curdgeon a job in Anchorage with Triple M, trying to get him into a milder climate. But Curdgeon had refused to take "charity," as he called it.

A sense of unreality crept over Mike as he approached the low building Curdgeon used as his home. From inside he could hear the silver lilt of Callie's laughter and the rusty sound of an old man chuckling. If Callie had gotten Curdgeon Post to laugh, it was the first time in recorded history.

"Callie?" Mike called, knocking on the door. "Everything checked out. We're ready to go."

The door swung open and Curdgeon scowled at him. "You best check that plane again. You ain't taking Calliope up where it ain't safe."

Mike stared, astonished. "It's safe."

"You should spend the night if yer not sure." Beneath Curdgeon's scowl, Mike saw a flicker of loneliness. Somehow Callie had reached the elderly man in a way no one else had been able to do.

"I'm certain it's all right. I'd never take a chance with Callie."

"Humph." He turned and shuffled to his chair by the woodstove, patting Callie's arm as he passed. "Yer man's here," he said quite unnecessarily.

She put her cup on a nearby table. "Thanks for the coffee."

"Weren't nothin'."

Callie motioned Mike over, and pointed to the radio. "We can get this frequency in Kachelak, right? Curdgeon and I want to talk. He's going to teach me the right codes and language to use as a dispatcher."

Mike felt the foundations of his world tremble. It was already shaky from hearing himself described as Callie's "man," and things were going downhill at a rapid pace. "That isn't necessary. We'll take care of it."

She smiled sunnily, at the same time digging an elbow into his side. "You're too busy, remember?"

"Oh, that's right."

Since he knew she had already mastered their radio, it was obviously just an excuse to stay in touch. Despite his shabby, rough exterior, she actually *liked* the old guy.

It was typical of Callie's loving heart. And it had nothing to do with being a preacher's daughter; she just cared about people—no matter how sexily she dressed or how many dates she made with other men. She didn't have a mean bone in her body.

"Well...we'd better get going," he murmured. "It's still a long way to Point Barrow."

"Okay. I'll send you those cookies as soon as I get a chance," Callie told her host.

"That'd be nice," said Curdgeon.

"You're going to cook?" Mike heard the hopeful note in his voice and he winced. He was not, repeat *not* desperate for home cooking—that might mean he wasn't happy with his bachelor life, which he was. *Very* happy. He loved being a bachelor and not having to worry about a wife nagging him.

"Don't worry, I won't mess up your kitchen," Callie assured him, but before he could protest that he didn't mind, she continued. "I've already arranged to bake them at Donovan's place—I promised him a batch, too."

Mike's eyes narrowed. Terrific. His partners were hogging her time, making moves like she was the last woman on earth, and *they* got to have cookies baked for them. It wasn't right—Callie was *his* friend, not theirs.

Well, technically she was Elaine's friend, but the only reason she'd come to Alaska was because she knew his family.

She ought to be spending more time with me.

Oh, yeah? And just who *tried to send her back to Washington,* his conscience prodded. *Or said you didn't have time to spend with her?*

Shut up, Mike ordered crossly. It didn't help to be honest; it was much easier being contrary.

Callie said goodbye to Curdgeon and followed Mike outside, fairly humming with energy. "What was wrong with the plane?" she asked when they were alone.

"Nothing. It was just a faulty gauge."

"Oh."

Something about the way she said "Oh" raised the hair on the back of Mike's neck. "Oh? What do you mean by that?"

"Nothing." Yet Callie chuckled nonetheless. "Is this the Alaskan version of 'running out of gas'?"

"What do you...*oh!*" Mike ground his teeth and glared at her. "I did *not* do it on purpose. I'm not a teenager, and I don't need an excuse to be alone with a woman."

"Don't worry, I won't tell."

"Callie!"

Laughing, she darted ahead and climbed into the back of the Comanche.

"What are you doing?"

"Getting my jacket. It's a little chilly."

Looking at her trim rear end, Mike felt anything but cold. "You...uh, seem to have gotten on Curdgeon's good side."

"He's a sweetie—all gruff on the outside and melted marshmallow on the inside."

"You're the only one who thinks so." Mike ran a finger inside his collar and tried to breathe. What was taking so long with that damned jacket? "Are you sure you brought a coat? Hell, just use mine."

"Of course I brought one," she said, her voice muffled as she pushed a suitcase to one side, her tight bottom wiggling with the effort. He counted to ten.

"Callie, about the plan. I didn't... A temp gauge *did* overheat, and that's why I put down here. Federal regulations require a pilot to set down when it happens."

"Sure. That's what all the guys say."

Mike climbed in behind her and grabbed her arm. "I'm not *all* the guys."

Callie peeked beneath her lashes and saw Mike's face, filled with frustration and the tiniest bit of desire. "Whatever you say, Mike."

He gave a wordless growl. "That...you're impossible."

"Think so?"

With a move so swift it startled her, he snatched her close and stared into her face. "I wish I knew what was going through that head of yours," he muttered thickly.

"Noth-nothing special."

"I'd like to believe that."

His palm cupped her face, while the other hand settled on her hip. Callie's pulse leapt, and it seemed as though time slowed, measured only by the heavy thud of her heart. The coffee, she thought faintly. It had been strong, black, with the consistency of syrup. No wonder her heart was behaving so wildly—drinking that much caffeine was like sending a locomotive through her system.

Mike's gaze lingered on her lips, and finally she flicked them with her tongue, unable to bear the suspense. He groaned and slid his thumb across her mouth. "Soft as velvet," he murmured.

She felt the warmth of his breath an instant before his kiss, a gentle exploration that made her breath catch. It was different than before. This time Mike was in control, not half-asleep or bombed with graduation revelry.

Sensual tremors swept through Callie at the butterfly caress. She wanted to think, to imprint the moment on her memory forever, but everything started turning fuzzy, lost in the rush of her blood.

"Open for me," he whispered, nibbling her bottom lip with the edge of his teeth.

It's too soon. Callie knew she shouldn't let things go so far, yet she needed Mike's touch with every shred of her being. She'd been patient all her life, and now when she needed that virtue more than ever, it was impossible to practice.

His eyes, dark and stormy, stared into hers as he waited.

Her lips parted on a sigh and he smiled with slow, burning triumph.

"That's it, sweet..."

The taste of mint and coffee mingled as his tongue circled hers. Intoxicating, a seamless joining filled with all kinds of promise. Waves of pleasure lapped at her senses. Every inch of her skin was tuned to his touch, and she yielded more to him with every second.

The world spun as he twisted with her in his arms, somehow managing to find room for them to lie in the cramped confines of the plane. She instinctively adjusted to his greater weight, unable to stop, any more than she'd been able to keep from loving him.

"Damn, Callie...what I am doing?"

Yes.

She wanted to hear her name, to know he was wholly aware it was *her* he held and kissed. Perhaps those kisses in the past belonged to a nameless, faceless body, but this one belonged to her alone.

Their legs tangled and Callie moaned, loving the sensation of hard, lean strength against her softness. A tingling ache spread from the center of her abdomen, pleading for release, and she tugged at the tails of his shirt.

She'd waited so long, she needed all of him—every powerful muscle and masculine angle. The buttons of his shirt parted, and she stroked her palms across the dark wedge of hair on his chest.

"Have to stop," Mike mumbled, yet his hands mirrored her own actions, sliding her T-shirt up and over her breasts. He trailed a series of nibbling kisses across her chin and throat and teased her silk-covered nipples with damp strokes of his tongue.

Callie shifted ever so slightly, the hooks of her bra coming loose as he tugged the thin piece of silk away from her body. Sighs and whispered kisses fell across her sensitized flesh, and she arched as he drew one taut crest into his mouth, rolling the other between his fingers. The muscles in her stomach clenched again and again, and she gasped, the restless ache turning into fire.

"I'm dreaming," she murmured, more to herself than the man who touched her so intimately. Mike started, a jolt of surprise that shook them both.

"Dream...?"

"Never mind," Callie whispered.

"I shouldn't...I've got to stop," he said again, his breathing labored and fast.

No...not yet.

Her hands swept over his shoulders, exploring their broad strength. If she didn't succeed...if Mike didn't fall in love with her, it might be the last time she ever touched him. The enormity of the risk she'd taken was never more clear; with each minute she fell more in love with Mike.

"Callie..."

"No, it's all right," she breathed.

All right?

No, Mike thought dimly. Callie was under his protection. She didn't understand about men.... Right now he was drawn so hard and tight he was ready to burst. Yet she tasted so sweet, he couldn't resist another loving taste, drawing first on the warm peaks of her breasts, then delving into the velvet depths of her mouth. She molded to him like fluid silk, resilient and generous in her response.

It's Callie, his mind screamed, but his body couldn't release her.

Not yet.

She was right; this was a dream. Soft and fragrant, filled with anticipation. He'd dreamt like this not long before, though it was just a shred of memory—he hadn't truly remembered until Callie had spoken.

Mike threaded his fingers through her hair—he loved the sensation as the streaks spilled in silken streams over everything. What would it be like in bed? Even as he thought the question, he knew. She'd shake her hair over him and burn him alive.

"I'm glad you never cut this," he muttered.

He was to the point of forgetting everything, when a chill breeze swept through the open door of the plane, curling around them both. Callie shivered, her nipples crinkling tighter, made even more vulnerable from the moisture left by his mouth.

Like a ghostly hand had tapped him on the shoulder, Mike jerked away and stared down at her.

Callie, but not Callie.

Her chestnut hair lay in a tangled cloud, mussed from his restless fingers. Her lips were red and swollen from hard kisses, and rosy-tipped breasts were taut with the response he'd drawn from her. Passion dazed her eyes, and he found himself blushing for the first time in years.

"I'm sorry." The hoarse rasp of his voice sounded strange, even to him.

The tip of Callie's tongue touched her upper lip, and a surge of heat swept through his groin. "About what?"

What?

The softly worded question made him doubt his sanity. Or Callie's. He'd practically made love to her, despite being tangled with their suitcases and the other gear he always carried on long hauls. Though he hadn't realized it before, they were jammed into the cargo section like a pair of sardines. An emergency kit was digging into his thigh, and Callie had to be even more uncomfortable with his tool bag beneath her shoulder.

None of it had mattered a minute ago; now it made him groan with self-disgust. Where was his subtlety? He hadn't gotten so out of control since high school. Most women would have been offended by the whole thing, but not Callie—*she* wanted to know what he was sorry about.

Mike swallowed and looked away from the tempting display of her breasts. "I—I didn't invite you on this trip to…uh…try anything like this."

Somehow he couldn't say "to *seduce* you." Callie wasn't the kind a woman you seduced. She was a preacher's daughter, and in his opinion, preacher's kids fell into two categories, hell-raisers or angels. And Callie definitely wasn't a hell-raiser.

Still, his gaze was drawn back to her, lying with unmoving grace amongst the tumbled luggage and packages. She hadn't scrambled to cover herself, or even blushed from embarrassment. She just lay there, watching him with eyes that had turned silvery green.

Enigmatic.

Seductive.

Well…she wasn't exactly an angel, either.

Shrugging out of his own jacket, Mike tucked it over Callie's exposed breasts. One of her eyebrows lifted, and she sat up, holding the garment in place.

"Haven't you ever seen a woman's body before?"

"Not yours," he mumbled. Callie wasn't just any woman, and she knew it. "We'd better get going— we're going to reach Barrow a lot later than we'd planned."

Callie sighed as Mike levered himself into the pilot's seat. He had wanted her, if only for a moment. She wasn't so naive she didn't recognize a fully aroused male. And yet he'd broken things off, just as quickly as they'd started.

Not that she wanted to make love for the first time in the crowded cargo space of a plane, but it was disheartening to realize how quickly he'd come to his senses. From everything she'd ever read, a man didn't voluntarily stop when he'd gotten that…enthusiastic.

Was it her?

Had she done something wrong? Surely he liked to be touched, as well. Callie looked down at her fingers, remembering the feel of Mike's hot skin beneath them…the rough silk of the hair on his chest and the flat disks of his nipples. She'd rasped them with her fingernails and his entire body had shuddered in response.

Callie shook her head. He'd *liked* the way she'd touched him; she'd stake her life on it. Men were impossible. And they thought women were unreasonable and hard to figure out.

"Curdgeon's coming out again. He probably wants to know if we're staying the night after all."

The terse warning brought her head up, and Callie scrambled to pull her clothes together. A belated heat filled her face as she realized Enoch Post might have seen them kissing. For good measure, she stuck her arms into Mike's large jacket and clutched the lapels together as she climbed into the seat next to him. She managed a small wave at the elderly man.

"What's goin' on? Thought you said there warn't no problem," Curdgeon said, eyeing Mike suspiciously.

"There isn't."

"That right, Calliope?"

Nothing a marriage license wouldn't solve, Callie mused silently. "Fine," she said out loud. "I was just looking for my coat and Mike was…helping me."

"All right. I'll be waitin' to hear from ya, like ya promised." The subtle quaver in his voice erased her self-consciousness, and she smiled warmly.

"We'll talk first thing on Monday morning. I want to know what happened to that bear after you hit him with a tree trunk."

Curdgeon guffawed. "Jist gave him a bit of a headache, that's all."

"That must have annoyed him. Tell me the rest when I call."

Curdgeon nodded and stepped back reluctantly.

Mike started the engine when Curdgeon had moved a safe distance way. Without a word, he turned the plane and took off, a stony expression on his face.

At the moment, Callie didn't know if she should be

happy or upset. She certainly didn't relish dissecting that kiss, or trying to explain why she'd returned it so ardently when she was supposed to be romantically interested in Donovan Masters or Ross McCoy.

Instead of teasing Mike, she should have been smart and stayed out of his arms. At the rate she was going, he'd probably fly her back to Washington...personally.

Callie sighed again, and wondered why every time she took one step forward, she lost several yards going back.

Chapter Six

The flight over the Brooks Range was accomplished in silence, Mike looking grimmer by the minute.

Callie prudently kept her mouth shut and stared at the austere landscape until her eyes burned. Fine, let Mike be the one to break the silence. See if she cared.

With such a late start and the delays, it was well after nine in the evening before they landed at the Barrow airport. It was light, of course. That far north the sun rose in May, and set sometime in August, their "day" actually lasting eighty-four days.

Except for a few terse words when they found a restaurant for a late dinner, Mike remained quiet. And when they finally checked into their motel, Callie escaped to her room with only a muttered good-night following her.

"I'll good night him," she grumbled, climbing into the shower for a long time. The hot water stung her skin, but it didn't erase the memory of his caresses.

She knew Mike had a lot to think about—it couldn't

be easy changing your understanding of a woman so quickly, yet her own heart was getting mangled in the process. Maybe she had been the poster child for small-town wholesomeness all her life, but that didn't mean she lacked sex appeal.

Callie put on pajamas, then lay on the bed, tapping her fingers on her stomach. They were in the newest motel in Barrow, and it was a nice room. Tomorrow she'd finally get to see polar bears in the wild and a completely different kind of life...except none of it really mattered.

Nothing had changed because of a kiss; she'd have to accept that and come up with a new strategy. And it wasn't as though she hadn't known the kiss was a mistake when it started—she had no one to blame but herself.

"Callie?" Mike's muffled voice was followed by a light tap on the door, and she sighed. "Are you still awake?"

She could have taken the coward's way out, but instead she got up and wrenched the door open. "Yes, I'm still awake. What do you want?"

"Uh..." Mike rubbed the back of his neck, looking too damned sexy and alive to ignore. "Listen, Callie. We should talk."

The inside of her mouth felt stuffed with dry cotton and she swallowed. "Maybe we should wait until to-morrow."

"No, I have to apologize. I feel terrible about what happened."

Callie's fingernails dug into her palm and she re-laxed with an effort. "Like I said, about what?"

"Sheesh, quit playing dumb. I shouldn't have

kissed you. It was wrong, and I'm sorry for letting
things get out of control.''

"Oh…I see." Her eyes narrowed. "You're taking
responsibility for what happened."

"Yes! You have every right to be upset. We're
friends and you should have been able to trust me."

Callie fought the temptation to scream. What business did Mike have, taking the ''blame?'' They'd
kissed, big deal. They were two healthy adults who
found each other attractive. At least she hoped he
found her attractive. Mike's feelings were hard to understand at this point.

"And what part did I play in this drama?" she
asked with deceptive calm. "I mean, was I just a helpless innocent, without any choice in the matter?"

"I didn't say that."

"You didn't have to."

Callie crossed her arms, ignoring the growing hurt
inside of her. Maybe Mike was having a problem sorting out his feelings, but she didn't deserve to be
treated like a child. In her heart, she'd been married
to Mike for a long time, so the morality of sleeping
with him outside of a legal ceremony didn't bother
her—at least not much.

But they'd only kissed, and now he acted like she
was a Victorian virgin who'd been ravished.

"For your information, Michael Fitzpatrick, I *do*
know something about men," she said angrily. "I
could have stopped you. Maybe I didn't move a thou-
sand miles away from Crockett, but I've dealt with
everything from muggers to groping CEOs."

Stunned, Mike just stared at her.

"I told you I was a management consultant. Did
you think I did that from the church office in Crockett?

No, I actually go to the big, bad city for my work. And it's amazing how many men think a consultant's fee includes a little sex on the side.''

The expression on his face turned murderous. ''That's outrageous.''

''Yes, it is. But for every groper, there's a decent guy who just wants to run his business better. Grow up, Mike. I have. Like it or not, there were two of us in that kiss, and you aren't any more 'responsible' for it than I am.''

''Callie, I didn't mean to hurt you.''

Ignoring his pleading tone, she turned away and Mike caught her arm. Waves of cold rolled from his skin, and she shivered. ''You're frozen. Did you go out for a walk?''

''No.'' He stepped in and closed the door, shutting out the curious eyes and ears of an eavesdropping couple in the hall.

''I don't recall inviting you into my room.''

''So? I didn't invite you to live with me, but you moved in anyway.''

''Huh. You insisted after Donovan asked. I could still stay with him, if that's what you want.''

''*No.*''

Mike slumped in the only chair and appeared to contemplate his shoes. His hair was damp and tousled, and Callie realized he must have showered, as well, before coming to ''apologize.''

A tiny smile tugged at her lips. A cold shower?

''What do you want, Mike?''

''I don't know.'' He sounded so baffled, she hurt for another reason.

''I...uh...'' Callie cleared her throat. ''If it helps, I wanted to kiss you, too.''

His head jerked up and he stared at her. "Why?"

"Why does any woman want to kiss a man? You're attractive, and we were friends…once. You must have been curious, and I felt the same." She shrugged, leaning back on the bed. "It doesn't mean anything—nothing happened. Besides, I miss being close to someone I care about."

A frown creased Callie's forehead as she thought about her answer. She *did* miss being close to someone. Maybe Keith hadn't been her soul mate, but she'd cared about him and missed the affection they shared—both physical and emotional. There were all kinds of love, and she would have made Keith happy; a lot of people settled for much less in their lives.

"What are you thinking about, Callie?" The softly worded question startled her and she blinked.

"About my fiancé."

"Your *what?*"

"I was engaged once…a long time ago."

The shock on Mike's face would have been funny, if it hadn't been so discouraging. Apparently he'd never thought of her getting married, or doing any of the usual things a woman did with her life.

A hollow sensation burrowed into her stomach. Sometimes it seemed useless, trying to make him see her as anything but the "nice" preacher's kid. She'd done a lot of living since he'd left Crockett, but he couldn't see that.

"When…that is, what happened?"

She sighed and lifted her shoulders. "He died in an accident, a few weeks before the wedding. I thought Elaine might have mentioned it to you."

Mike's internal gyroscope wobbled and he clutched the arms of the chair. Callie married…*almost* married?

Her fiancé killed in an accident? Frantically he searched his memory for anything Elaine might have said, disgusted that he might have been so insensitive he'd forgotten the tragedy.

He loosened his flannel overshirt, suddenly warm despite his icy shower; it had been the only way he could face Callie without losing control again. Who would have imagined she could turn him on so quick and hard? He still ached with frustration and need, no matter how long he'd stood under that frigid shower.

"I met Keith at the university," Callie said, almost to herself. "We took the same class in our senior year, and before long we spent all our time together. He could make me laugh so hard, I'd think nothing in the world could go wrong. But it did, and life went on."

Mike shifted in the chair, wanting to offer comfort, but not knowing how. He felt like a crumb—if the situation was reversed, Callie would have known what to do...maybe just by offering a kind word and a hug.

At the moment, he didn't dare hug Callie; he didn't know how well he could control himself. Comforting might turn into something a lot more passionate, and that would lead to a lot of complications he didn't want to think about.

"I don't remember...er...getting an invitation to the wedding."

"You didn't." A smile edged with wry humor quirked her lips. "At the time you were working on the Alaska pipeline, and nobody knew how to reach you."

"Oh."

There was a reason he hadn't heard about Callie's engagement, or her fiancé's accident. He'd been saving every penny, trying to save a stake for his own company, so he'd been out of touch except for an occasional phone call home.

"I'm sorry," he said gently.

"So am I."

Sorrow and acceptance shadowed her eyes, yet she'd never looked more beautiful. Silky, dark blue pajamas draped the delicate lines of her body, the perfect foil for her chestnut hair. She'd only buttoned two of the buttons, leaving a creamy white patch of skin exposed at her waist. At the same time, lace edging drew attention to the curves of her breasts, molded by the soft fabric.

She had to be aware of how provocative she looked, yet she didn't make a move to put on a robe or cover herself. She just lay there, like she had in the plane after they'd kissed—comfortable with her sensuality.

Hell-raiser or angel?

If she wasn't either one, what did that leave?

A woman.

The insistent voice hammered in his head. And though he still had a niggling discomfort with the idea, Mike couldn't deny that Callie was a very *desirable* woman.

"I'd better leave, so you can sleep," he muttered hoarsely. "I'll see you in the morning."

"In the morning," she echoed as he strode to the door. At the last minute he glanced back and saw her stretching, the movement straining the two buttons she had fastened on the pajama top.

Another cold shower, he decided hastily...and wondered if there was enough ice in the Arctic to cool him down.

The door closed behind Mike as Callie stretched again and savored the tingle inside her body. If she wasn't mistaken, he had taken a good look at her. With new eyes.

Maybe the kiss hadn't been such a mistake after all.

Now that he'd realized she was more than a child, he might fall in love with her. Finally. They'd be so good together—not just in bed, but in other ways.

Still... Mike's restraint bothered Callie. She didn't plan to spend her life being treated like an innocent child. Intimacy wasn't the most important part of a relationship, but it was important.

Granted, at the moment she was little crazy from being in the middle of her monthly cycle. Her hormones were screaming "go for it" so loud, it was hard to think about anything else. Hormones could be very demanding, especially when the biological clock was ticking. She wanted to make a baby with Michael Fitzpatrick and she didn't appreciate his stubborn self-control in the matter.

From the other side of the wall her room shared with Mike's, she heard the shower go on.

More cold water?

In Barrow, even summer temperatures averaged at near freezing temperatures, so their cold water was really cold.

Callie turned over and smiled faintly. Apparently, her hormones weren't the only ones screaming for attention.

Mike rolled over on the bed and rubbed his throbbing temples. He hadn't slept more than twenty minutes at a stretch, thanks to Callie. Each time he'd closed his eyes, he'd remembered the taste of her mouth, or how she felt as she arched against him.

I did the right thing, stopping, he insisted silently. It wouldn't have been right making love to Callie, no matter how incredible kissing her might be.

"Damnation," Mike muttered, getting up to splash water on his face. On top of everything else, the few times he'd actually fallen asleep, he'd dreamed a series of steamy, sensual images from his past.

Like that kiss from college.

Or that other dream. He'd remembered finally; he'd had it the night Callie first arrived. Now *that* had been a great dream. Hot and sexy, with all the right ingredients except a great ending.

And they were all mixed up with kissing Callie.

Mike shook his head, water dripping from his chin. It didn't make sense. Why connect the three kisses, one of which wasn't even real?

Or was it?

He wiped the water from his face and walked back into the bedroom, a frown growing between his eyes. Callie couldn't have kissed him that first night in Alaska, could she? He recalled the way she'd looked after her date with Donovan—her hair wild, and eyes filled with exhilaration.

He wouldn't have minded kissing her, even then. He just kept stumbling over his mental image of her as the preacher's daughter. Crockett was a nice, old-fashioned town that did things a certain way—like have certain ideas about the preacher's family. Cripes, his own father would have gone after him with a baseball bat if he'd ever looked at Callie Webster that way.

Of course, they were both adults now.

The phone rang abruptly and he picked it up. "Yes?"

"Are you up?"

Mike couldn't help grinning, though the "up" Callie meant probably wasn't intended as a double entendre. "I've been up most of the night."

"Can't sleep when there's daylight outside? Did you take all those showers for relaxation?"

The little witch. He didn't know how much practical experience she possessed, but her mind had a healthy sexual awareness.

"How do you know I took showers...plural?"

Her laugh shimmered through the line. "Your room is next to mine, and the walls aren't that thick."

"Oh. Then you know I was alone."

"Are you that noisy...when you have company?"

Mike swallowed a groan. He shouldn't be playing this game with her; he didn't know the rules. Actually, he had the feeling Callie was writing the rules as she went along. More than likely, she was only flirting with him because Donovan and Ross weren't around; she obviously preferred their company.

The thought was unreasonably depressing.

"Mike?"

"Never mind about noisy company. Let's go to breakfast, so we can get out to see your polar bears."

"I've already eaten, but I have a breakfast sandwich waiting for you...and some coffee. If you don't mind," she said in a coaxing tone. "I've been awake for hours."

Since it was the closest he'd probably get to having her cook for him, Mike accepted. "Okay, I'll meet you out front in ten minutes."

"You could eat in my room."

The memory of Callie reclining on her bed made Mike's body clench. *"No."*

"Coward."

"I prefer to think of it as prudent."

She laughed again and said goodbye.

Mike sighed and stumbled back to the sink to splash more water on his face. He'd be lucky to survive this trip. Clearly, he needed to rebuild his defenses against Callie.

She's an old friend, nothing more.

Right, and he was a moose's rear end.

Those defenses would be hard to rebuild, he decided dismally. But if he didn't want to be a blithering, drooling candidate for an insane asylum, he'd better get busy. Callie needed someone who wanted to get married, and no matter how much she turned him on, he didn't have any intention of proposing.

Six hours later Mike checked the altimeter and took a sip of cooling coffee. Callie sat curled into a ball beside him, asleep despite the noise from the engine.

It wasn't any surprise she was exhausted. Neither of them had slept the night before, and she'd been so excited to see her polar bears. They'd even spotted a baby, romping about on the ice with youthful exuberance.

He loved that part of Callie—her enthusiasm for life. Even when they were kids and she had adult-size responsibility in the church, she'd laugh and make everything seem fun. He'd been thinking about that a lot lately.

Reaching into the rear area, he pulled a blanket out and shook it over her.

"Aren't you tired?" she asked without opening her eyes.

"I'll manage. Go back to sleep."

Callie turned in the seat and blinked. "I should keep you company, help you stay awake."

"Naw, I'll be fine. I do this all the time."

Her fingers curled around the edge of the blanket, a drowsy smile on her lips. "Tough guy, huh?"

Mike laughed. "That's right."

She yawned and murmured something else, so groggy he wasn't sure if she'd remember waking up at all. A warm spot grew around his heart. He liked taking care of her.

In a way, Callie was *too* independent. Warning her away from Donovan and Ross had just put her back up, making her determined to continue dating the two men.

Mike grimaced—he should have kept his mouth shut. Callie didn't appreciate his interference, and he wasn't sure himself why it seemed important to keep her away from his partners. In the future he'd just have to bite his tongue and trust the two men; they were decent guys who would never force her into something she didn't want.

He looked at Callie again and tucked the blanket in tighter against the high-altitude chill. He'd never force her into anything, either, but he sure wondered what it would be like to kiss her again.

"We'll have that shipment to you by the end of the week," Callie assured, and placed the receiver back on the hook.

The weekend was over, and Mike had retreated to a casual sociability—a far cry from the previous day, loaded with sensual glances and silences charged with awareness.

One step forward, a mile back.

Callie glared at the innocent computer and typed a final formula into the program. Like it or not, she was dragging Triple M Transit into the computer age. They'd expanded to the point it was a miracle the company hadn't crashed and burned on their antiquated bookkeeping system.

It's the Alaska way, they'd all protested.

Ha.

She didn't think it had anything to do with Alaska, just the medieval male brains at the controls. If Triple M ever got audited, they'd better just cross their fingers and pray.

"Hey, *beautiful.*"

She looked up and smiled. "Hi, Ross. How's your head?"

"Attached...barely. I don't get migraines often, but when I do, I'm out for the count. Sorry I couldn't take you to Barrow."

"That's okay—Mike took me instead."

Ross sat on the desk and wiggled his eyebrows. "And how did that go?"

"The jury is still out." She took a stack of invoices from a folder and began entering figures into the newly created database. This way she'd be able to track expenses and profits, and a multitude of information that Mike and company had always handled manually.

To be fair, they'd actually done very well without her help. It was amazing the amount of information Mike and the others carried around in their heads, then entered into old-style ledger books.

"Sorry to hear it."

"No, you're not," Callie teased, her hands flying across the keyboard. "If I succeed too quickly, you'll lose your entertainment for the summer."

He snapped his fingers. "Oh, right. How could I forget?"

They were laughing as Mike walked into the room and frowned. Callie turned pink and hastily entered another set of figures into the computer.

Mike narrowed his eyes, looking between his partner and Callie. She hadn't blushed when *he'd* kissed her, or even when she'd been practically topless in the plane. Two explanations immediately sprang to mind, and he didn't like either one of them.

One, she and Ross were intimately involved, and he'd made a suggestion that made her flush with passion.

Or two, she was too comfortable with her "old buddy Mike" to feel any embarrassment about being...exposed. Comfortable, like an old shoe. The disposable cup he held suddenly split from the pressure of his fingers, hot coffee splashing everywhere.

"Yeow!"

"Mike, are you all right?"

Callie grabbed a handful of tissues and dabbed his hand, her gentle concern so much like the "old" Callie that he ached. The weather had turned cooler, and today she wore jeans and a sweatshirt, a common enough outfit from their childhood. Only after a steamy kiss and a painful two weeks of getting his eyes pried open, he couldn't see the child anymore.

"Mike? Are you burned?" she asked insistently.

He shook himself from his trance and flexed his fingers. "Not a chance—I'm a tough guy."

"Oh, please. Spare me."

Taking his hand, she bent her head and examined his skin for signs of injury. The sweet warmth of her breath burned more than the hottest coffee and he gritted his teeth. Ross smiled pityingly from a few feet away, though it wasn't clear who was on the receiving end of his sympathy...or why.

Mike gave him a lethal glance and looked back at Callie. Lately, the subtle fragrance of her perfume haunted him...and haunted his dreams. After a day of thinking, he was certain she *had* kissed him her first day in Alaska, though her motives were still a mystery.

Hell, everything about Callie was a mystery, so what hope did he have of figuring out why she'd kiss him in the first place? Or why he'd want her so badly, when she was just a nice kid from his hometown.

"Are you sure you aren't burned?" she asked. "I can get some ointment from the first-aid kit."

He cleared his throat. "It wasn't that hot. For heaven's sake, you don't have to fuss like a mother hen. I'm not one of your Sunday school kids."

Callie instantly dropped his hand. She stepped back in haste, slipping on the coffee he'd spilled. Simultaneously both Ross and Mike leapt to catch her and she gasped as she was jostled between their much-larger bodies.

They stepped back, apologizing profusely and she slapped their supportive hands away.

"I'm fine, Mike. Leave me alone. I don't need a 'mother hen' any more than you do."

Mike winced. He didn't blame Callie for wanting to be left alone; at the moment he didn't particularly relish his own company. He grabbed Ross's arm. "Come on."

"She said you, buddy, not me."

"I don't care."

Mike shoved his partner through the side door and into the hangar, unreasonably jealous because Callie didn't want his help, while Ross's had been welcome. And it was his own fault. He'd deliberately been unkind, trying to conceal his reaction to her touch.

"Do you have to act like a jackass all the time?" Ross snarled. "Callie is great for the company. We need her to stay, and I, for one, am willing to do whatever it takes to keep her."

Mike stared, remembering the night Ross had come to pick Callie up for their date. *Callie's a grown woman, and she'd make some guy a great wife.*

Wife.

The thought made him see red. Good, old-fashioned jealousy—so much for trusting his friends. He might as well be honest; he didn't want to get involved with Callie, but he didn't want Ross or Donovan involved with her, either.

"Don't even think about it," Mike warned softly. Ross and Donovan could think about wedding rings and wedding nights all they pleased, just not with Callie.

"That's between Callie and me."

"Stop it, both of you," Donovan ordered from where he was inspecting a plane. "You're acting like two of the Three Stooges."

"Yeah, and who's elected to be the third stooge?" Mike snapped.

Donovan just smiled. "Go ahead and screw it up, pal. I thought you were too smart to ruin a good thing, but I must have been wrong."

Mike thrust his hand out, his thumb and forefinger held a scant inch apart. "You're this close, pal."

"Yeah? And how close are you?"

Muttering a vicious curse, Mike wheeled around. He had an overnight junket scheduled to California and should have left already. The only reason he'd gone into the office was to say goodbye.

Now Callie was mad at him, and he'd be out of state while Ross and Donovan stuck around Kachelak. They didn't have any flight time scheduled for another three days—it was one of the perks of owning a prosperous business. After years of eighteen-hour days they'd been able to cut back.

Briefly, Mike wished the Triple M hadn't gotten so successful. That way, none of them would have had time to spend with Callie.

But no, while his partners romanced Callie, he was scheduled to pick up a group of chatty businessmen, willing to shell out big money for private chauffeur services and a taste of Alaskan wilderness. His only consolation was knowing they'd be Travis Black's problem once they arrived in Alaska—Travis being the Triple M's expert wilderness guide.

"See you in a couple days," Ross called. "I'll be sure to keep Callie company."

It was the last straw.

Mike turned, walked to Ross and slapped the flight plan into the other man's hand. "That won't be possible—you're going to be out of state. I'll see you in a couple of days. Have a good time in California."

A hard smile creased Ross's mouth. "What if I refuse to go?"

Mike rocked forward on the balls of his feet and returned the smile. "Trust me, you don't want to know."

Chapter Seven

Callie grabbed some rags from the closet and threw them over the spilled coffee.

You don't have to fuss like a mother hen. I'm not one of your Sunday school kids.

The rat.

If she'd had a knife, she would have stuck it right between Mike's ribs. So it was probably lucky there hadn't been a knife in sight.

Maybe she had fussed, but it wasn't a crime; when you cared about someone you didn't want them to hurt. As for the Sunday school crack, she could just scream. They'd finally shared a passionate, fully conscious and *sober* kiss over the weekend, and the first thing that popped into his head was the fact she used to teach Sunday school.

It seemed hopeless.

Still furious, she scrubbed every trace of moisture from the ugly linoleum floor. *It's* really *ugly,* she thought, looking down, *and worn-out.* It had to go.

Her next step was getting Mike, Ross and Donovan to refurbish the place. But at least it was clean, and an additional phone line had been installed, along with a sophisticated answering machine.

"Callie?"

Callie pressed her lips together and plunked herself down at the computer. She wasn't too fond of Mike at the moment; it would be safer if he stayed a good distance away from her.

"Hey, Callie."

"Go away."

"I'm sorry."

Ha. She didn't care how many apologies Mike offered. He was an impossible, egotistical wretch, and she wanted him to suffer. Or at least to marry her— *then* she'd make him suffer. Every night, in bed. She'd torment him by being the sexiest, most insatiable wife a man ever had.

A reluctant smile tugged the corners of Callie's mouth and she glanced at Mike from the corner of her eye. Drat, she couldn't stay angry with him, not when he had that little-boy, gosh-I'm-pond-slime expression on his face.

"I seem to be apologizing a lot lately." He tugged a lock of her hair. "I'm really sorry. It was nice of you to worry about me getting burned."

Hmm.

"Aren't you supposed to be on your way to California?" she asked after an acceptable period of silence.

"Ross decided to go instead. Hear that? He's getting ready for takeoff."

The roar of the Piper Comanche drifted through the

open window and Callie shook her head. "I don't understand. Ross doesn't like tourists."

"He'll manage."

"You made him go, didn't you?" Callie accused.

"I don't know what you mean—we're partners. Equal voting power... How could I force him to go anywhere?" Mike gave her a charming smile that didn't fool her for an instant. He sat on a corner of the desk, which was the only place to sit in the office besides her own chair.

"You need more places to sit in here," she said. "How do you hold board meetings in this office?"

"We don't. We just sit around on oil drums in the hangar."

"That I believe. You need to think about expanding—for starters, you need more support staff. This isn't a one-plane operation anymore."

"I know. We've managed because so many of the cargo shipments are on regular runs. But since we've become involved in the tourist trade—it's gotten a lot more complicated." He reached over and casually tucked a strand of hair behind her ear.

Trying to breathe normally, Callie concentrated on sorting the receipts she'd found from April. It wouldn't be good to let Mike know her pulse doubled whenever he was nearby. Right now, her advantage lay in letting him think she wasn't truly interested...in him.

"Shouldn't you be doing something—like working on a plane, or running Donovan out of the state?" she asked after several minutes when Mike didn't say anything.

"Do I need to run Donovan out of the state?" The

question sounded lazy, but the look in his eyes was anything but lazy.

"I thought we settled all of this." Callie took out the current week's flight schedule and erased Mike's name on the California tourist run, replacing it with Ross's. "Whatever happens is between me and them. Now you can leave." She glared and pointed to the door. "I've got better things to do than sit around while you play the overbearing big brother. Honestly, do you think sending Ross to California will change anything?"

"No," Mike admitted sourly.

He hadn't thought at all, not beyond wanting to punch one of his two best friends in the face. That's what a woman did to a man—she turned him into a maniacal ass. And it wasn't even like he wanted Callie himself...not really. Maybe she'd grown up and become a sexy armful, but he wasn't the right man for her.

Besides, she had to have as much trouble seeing him in a romantic fashion as he had seeing her that way.

The thought stopped him dead.

Callie might have enthusiastically participated in that kiss, but she mostly treated him just like a brother. And having Callie see him as a big brother wasn't terribly appealing anymore.

Mike jumped to his feet. He needed to think.

"Wait. The least you can do is drop these at the post office," Callie said. She held out a neat bundle of mail containing billings to customers, and an advertising flyer they'd completed the week before.

"Yeah...sure." Mike strode from the office and took several deep breaths.

What was making him so nuts?

It had to be the kiss, except kissing Callie couldn't have been so great, not even close to that knockout kiss from college.

Grow up.

You know it was fantastic.

Mike rubbed the back of his neck. Okay, he admitted it. He wanted to kiss Callie again and figure out why she turned him on so much. After a long winter a man got…restless. Maybe his judgment had been skewed by that, or maybe she was as hot as he thought.

Either way, he had to figure out how to manage it. He hadn't exactly endeared himself to Callie, and she didn't seem to be in a forgiving frame of mind.

It was after four when Callie decided to brave the company storeroom. Until then she'd been able to ignore the dusty space through sheer willpower. But when the third mouse ran through the office, across her sneakers and into the washroom, she decided it couldn't wait any longer.

Taking off her sweatshirt, Callie started clearing a path through the crowded storage space, hoping she'd find the mouse's home before she was asphyxiated by dust.

"Want some dinner?" Donovan asked an hour later.

Callie backed out of the storeroom, shaking her head and coughing. "Nope, I'm headed for a hot bath. Don't you guys ever throw anything away?" She held up a bag of *National Geographic* magazines. Bits of shredded paper sifted the top like confetti, thanks to several generations of mouse families having made it their nest.

"Never know what you'll need someday."

"Yeah, right."

"Come on, we'll go to dinner and—"

"Jeez!" With a shriek Callie dropped the sack and swatted at her arm. Two more mice ran from the spilled magazines, disappearing between Donovan's feet.

"Did one of them jump on you?"

"No…it was a spider." Callie checked her arm anxiously, just in case the arachnid had taken up residence behind her elbow. "Where did he go?"

"Let me take a look," Donovan offered with a significant look toward the window. Mike's Dodge Dakota was just pulling up outside and Callie grinned.

"That's so kind."

Impulsively she lifted up on her toes and gave him a kiss. They were nice, Mike's partners. It would have been much less complicated falling in love with one of them.

"Phew! Honey, if you weren't a one-man woman, you'd be perfect." Donovan took her hand and put one hand on her waist while he examined her arm, then her shoulder and neck with apparent intimacy.

"Callie?" Mike's outraged voice echoed in the room.

She looked over Donovan's broad shoulder into his glowering face. "Oh. Hi, Mike."

"What's going on?"

"What do you think?" Donovan asked lazily.

The look exchanged between the two men was filled with hostility and Callie groaned. She wasn't good at this vamp stuff; her conscience kept getting in the way. "A spider startled me, that's all. Donovan offered to make sure it wasn't still on me."

"And you believed him?"

"Funny, she takes mice in her stride, but doesn't like spiders at all," Donovan said conversationally as he plucked a cobweb from her shoulder. "Enjoy your hot bath, Callie. I'll see you in the morning."

At the words *hot bath*, Mike's breath hissed through his teeth. "No, you won't. I'm taking her to climb Kachelak Glacier tomorrow."

Callie's eyes narrowed. "Michael Fitzpatrick, it would be nice if you *invited* me before making plans. Anyway, you don't have time to—"

"Stop throwing that in my face," he growled. "I was wrong, all right? I'm making the time."

"Don't do me any favors. Besides, I can't take a day off in the middle of the week. I've got work to do. And what about taking cargo orders and scheduling charters?"

"So?" Mike snapped his fingers. "That's one of the reasons we got an answering machine, to cover things when we're not in the office. You've done a ton of work and you deserve an extra day off. Right, partner?"

Donovan gave her a surreptitious wink as he gathered up the magazines she'd dropped and strolled to the exit. "Whatever you say."

Mike ground his teeth, but there wasn't anything to protest when Donovan was agreeing with him. What a muddle. He wasn't sure what he'd interrupted, or if he'd interrupted anything between Callie and the other man.

"Callie—"

"I've started cleaning the storeroom," she said brightly, as though he hadn't found her in the middle of...something. "I hope you don't have any special attachment to the stuff in there, because I'm throwing most of it out.''

''Not really. A lot of it was there when we bought the place. Callie, about Don—''

''How long ago was that?''

Mike sighed. ''Eight years.''

She shook her head. ''And men say women are pack rats.'' She took out a broom and started sweeping the floor.

He cleared his throat and tried again. ''I saw you kiss Donovan.''

''So? I kissed you and it didn't mean anything.''

''It meant something,'' Mike said grimly. Damned if he could decide *what* it meant, particularly since he didn't want to get married, even to Callie. And as much as he'd love having an affair, he wasn't berserk enough to imagine having one with the preacher's daughter.

Of course…if he kissed her again, he might *get* that berserk. He'd just have to rely on discretion and self-control. Maturity. A man with thirty-four years of living under his belt should be able to keep things from going too far.

''I meant what I said about climbing the glacier,'' he murmured, watching her graceful motions as she swept bits of paper into a dustpan. ''And I borrowed some hiking boots, in case you don't have any.''

She looked at him doubtfully. ''What size?''

''Six…I called Elaine. I also picked up some new ones for you, but I don't want you to get blisters breaking them in.''

''That's nice of you.'' Callie's lashes swept down, hiding her thoughts.

Mike frowned. Once, he would have said Callie was

the most uncomplicated girl he'd ever known. Yet that "uncomplicated" girl had turned into a woman who made his head spin. Maybe she'd always been a mystery, and he'd just been too blind to notice.

We've known each other forever. No thunderbolts here.

Callie was wrong. There *were* some thunderbolts. And just because they were childhood friends, it didn't mean they weren't sexually compatible.

"So, will you go?"

She emptied the dustpan into the garbage and shrugged. "I guess."

"Wow, your enthusiasm overwhelms me."

"Good." Callie grabbed her purse and keys. "Just so you understand, I can see Alaska just fine without your help. Ross already offered to take me glacier climbing."

"Right." Irritated, Mike locked the office behind them and followed her outside. "Ross wanted to go on a two-day trip to show you Worthington Glacier. But the funny thing is, we have one just a few miles away. It's not famous like Worthington or Portage, but you don't need to spend the night to see a glacier."

Callie climbed into the seat of the truck she'd borrowed from Ross. "We would have had separate motel rooms," she said tartly. "Just like in Barrow. Who would have thought you'd turn out to be so old-fashioned?"

Okay, he deserved that.

But no matter what Callie said, she was old-fashioned, too. Hell, it was hard escaping your hometown roots. He should know. For years he'd prided himself on getting away from Crockett, where couples married young and were old before they reached thirty.

Settled.

He didn't want to be settled.

Yet, here he was, with his propriety all offended, because Ross McCoy had wanted to take the preacher's daughter on a two-day glacier climbing trip. It just proved the old adage—you could take the boy out of the small town, but you couldn't take the small town out of the boy.

God, that was awful.

He thrust his hands in his pockets. "Look, I may have acted like a jerk when you arrived, but I don't want you to get hurt."

Her breath hissed out between her teeth. "I can take care of myself, Mike. Cripes, this isn't the nineteenth century. Even if I wanted to sleep with Ross, it wouldn't be any of your business."

He scowled, mostly because he didn't want Callie talking about having sex with Ross, even hypothetically. "That's not what I meant."

"Yeah, right. I'm going home," she said, starting the engine. "It's been a long day."

Mike opened his mouth to say he'd get some dinner, but she'd already pulled out of the parking lot. He sighed. Things weren't going the way he'd planned for the summer. On the other hand, it wasn't boring.

Or lonely.

Shaking his head, Mike got into his Dodge Dakota. Why would he think about being lonely? He didn't mind the isolation in Alaska, or the quiet winters. His life was going exactly the way he'd always planned. Maybe Curdgeon Post was lonely, but not Mike Fitzpatrick.

At least not much.

* * *

The alarm went off at five the next morning, and Mike slapped it off with a groan. Waking up was never easy, even during the summer when the sun rose just after 3:00 a.m. Rolling over, he took a deep breath and his eyes shot wide open.

Coffee.

The scent of coffee filled the air.

Grabbing his jeans, he pulled them on and stumbled toward the kitchen. The aroma of fresh-brewed java drifting ahead of him like a mirage.

"That smells wonderful."

Callie looked up from her book and hid a smile. No one could ever call Mike a morning person. "There's plenty, and I've fixed a thermos to bring on our hike."

"You're a lifesaver." Mike poured an enormous cup and took a big gulp. "Say, this is great."

"It's just coffee."

He pried his eyes open farther. "Sacrilege."

She let him savor his caffeine, happy to watch. Hair rumpled, chest bare, and his black jeans with only one metal button fastened, he was too much of a man not to demand attention. As a matter of fact, he fit right into Alaska with its tough and hardy reputation. She didn't know where restraint fit into the package, but she wished he had a little less of it.

A *lot* less.

It was discouraging. A part of her wanted a man who'd make love in the back of a plane, throwing caution and modesty to the wind. The other part wanted a husband...with all the sweet and tender and passionate moments mixed up together.

She shivered and took a sip from her own cup. "Do you want some leftover pizza for breakfast?" She motioned to the box sitting on the table."

Mike groaned. "It's too early for food."

Though she was still upset, Callie smiled again. Mike had brought the pizza the night before…all apologetic and sweet, laughing at himself and inviting her to share. If she hadn't already been in love, she would have fallen all over again.

However annoying, that protective streak of his was also endearing. It just got in the way of him seeing her as a woman, because it was Callie Webster, the preacher's daughter, he worried about protecting. She got up to put the pizza back in the refrigerator, but Mike caught her arm.

"Today…let's pretend we're two strangers, going on a date," he murmured.

This was promising. She dropped the box on the table to fully concentrate. "Yeah?"

His thumb circled the base of her wrist. "I've been thinking…."

Callie's heart slowed, then quickened. "That's dangerous."

"Quiet, woman." Yet he grinned, his slow, sexy grin that turned her inside out. "We should forget about knowing each other as kids and concentrate on the present."

"Oh…you mean, get to know the real Michael Fitzpatrick? The innovative entrepreneur, who's intelligent but stubborn as a Missouri mule? The guy who's illogical, hot-tempered and—"

"Don't forget attractive," he interjected.

Her eyebrows rose. "I was planning to add 'arrogant.'"

"Hey, you were the one who said I was attractive. Remember? At the motel the other night, when you admitted you wanted to kiss me, too."

Sheesh, she'd known that confession would come back to haunt her. Callie shrugged. "Okay, you're attractive. *And* arrogant."

"Anything else?"

There were plenty of things she could add, but she wasn't that stupid. After their last kiss, she didn't plan on throwing herself at Mike unless she was pretty sure he planned to catch her. There were more prudent ways of getting what she wanted.

"Callie?"

"Well, you're a good pilot."

He threaded their fingers together and tugged until she was sitting on his lap. "I'm glad you like something about me."

The temptation to slide deeper into his arms was overwhelming, but Callie gritted her teeth and kept her spine in a straight line instead of melting all over him. She couldn't risk spoiling everything for a temporary moment of gratification.

"I like you, Mike. I've always liked you," she said with a casual smile.

He shook her gently. "That's not playing along. We just met, remember? Two strangers going on a date."

Hmm. She didn't know how far he wanted to play that game, but it still seemed promising.

"How about it?" he prodded.

Callie balanced her arm on Mike's shoulder and looked him over. Dark beard stubble covered his jaw and except for his jeans, he wasn't wearing a stitch of clothing. She tried not to look too carefully at his southern hemisphere, but that half was promising, as well.

"I'll try, if you will," she said finally. "So, stranger, when are we headed for Kachelak Glacier?"

"As soon as we're dressed. And it'll have to be warm clothing—I don't want you freezing to death."

"Not a chance...I'm too hot-blooded."

"Must be that red hair."

Mike curled a lock of her hair around his finger, tugging sensually, and she realized something had changed. Whatever Mike had in mind, he wasn't puzzled anymore. In a subtle, undefined way, he'd taken command.

She blinked. "It's not red."

"Looks red in this light."

Glancing down, she saw Mike's hand a scant inch from her breast. Abruptly she slid from his legs and grabbed the pizza again. "I'd better get this in the fridge."

"Right." Mike drew a deep breath and tried to recover from the rush her slide had given him. At the moment he wasn't well protected, and her fanny had swiped a particularly vulnerable portion of his anatomy.

It would have been okay, except she'd gotten out of reach too quickly.

He was nuts.

How could he have asked Callie to pretend they were strangers, when all he could think about was tossing her over his shoulder and hauling her up to his bedroom? Now that would have impressed her with his finesse and restraint.

"Are you coming, or do you need more coffee?" Callie asked, pausing at the door.

"Uh...go ahead," he muttered. "I'll be up in a minute."

She disappeared down the hall and he sighed with relief. A man's body wasn't built to hide his response to a woman. Not that Callie would be embarrassed. At least, he didn't think she'd be embarrassed. She'd probably just raise her eyebrows, smile that enigmatic smile of hers and make him crazier than ever.

Hell, he was an idiot to go anywhere with Callie.

She made a man start thinking about home-cooking and baby carriages...and about the way you made babies to *go* in those carriages. He thought about that part a lot. If he wasn't careful, he'd end up married, like everyone else he'd grown up with in Crockett, Washington.

Married.

Hog-tied. Stuck to one woman forever.

Mike scowled...mostly because the idea wasn't nearly as awful as he'd always supposed.

Chapter Eight

"*Umpf!*"

"Having fun?"

Callie looked up from where she lay sprawled on the ice and raised an eyebrow. "I'm having a ball. Can't you tell?"

Mike was obviously trying not to laugh, and she appreciated his efforts. He held out a hand and helped her climb to her feet.

"Did you bruise anything?"

"Only my pride." Callie dusted bits of surface snow from her jeans. They'd been hiking over the ice field when she'd slipped and fallen on her backside.

Though relatively small, the glacier was too vast to fully comprehend, the implicit power in the frozen river making words like *beautiful* seem inadequate. Twisted, cracked and densely packed, the ice would take years to move more than a few feet, both shaping and shaped by the mountain as it went.

She shivered with awe.

When she and Mike were dead and buried, and their children had become old men and women, the glacier would still be here.

Sunlight scattered across the crevices and spires, shimmering with a spectral pale blue. Callie lifted her sunglasses and put them on again. After a few hours of climbing across the brilliant expanse, she understood how a skier could get snow blindness.

"Doing okay?" Mike adjusted his backpack, then tucked the edges of a scarf inside her collar.

"Fine. It's really not that cold."

"Tell me that when we've been out here longer."

"The voice of experience. How often do you come up?"

Mike grinned. "Only when I have a curious office manager who wants to see glaciers and polar bears."

Callie wrinkled her nose. "I happen to know you also brought Elaine up here, and at least one other time you came with your parents."

"You wouldn't know that if you were a stranger."

"I wouldn't be here, either." She gave him an assessing, and purely impudent look. "You aren't the reliable type."

"Sure. That's why you made me carry our lunch."

She rolled her eyes. They'd fought over the backpack, with Mike declaring he couldn't let a woman carry it, and Callie claiming it was an equal world and she didn't expect him to do all the work.

Mike had won.

But only because he was bigger, stronger and had longer arms. Her five-foot-four frame was at a distinct disadvantage when it came to a physical contest between the two of them.

Of course, there'd been a moment when she almost

won, when Mike had her squashed between his body and the Dakota and his eyes had dilated to the point she could hardly see any brown in them. To test her theory, she'd wriggled against him and been distinctly pleased with the result.

After that, who cared about women's lib and carrying a backpack?

She supposed the only reason Mike hadn't kissed her was because of the four teenagers who'd been hiking by, whistling and clapping. It tended to put a damper on the mood.

Drat.

The timing still wasn't right for another kiss, but she was getting flexible on that point.

"No comment?" Mike's mischievous smile said he remembered that moment by the Dakota, as well.

She shrugged and settled the sunglasses more firmly on her nose. "If you want to be an atavistic, regressed male and do all the work, who am I to deny you the pleasure?"

"I love it when you compliment me."

"Brawn over brains—you *would* think it was a compliment. Let's get going."

Mike stayed close, helping her over the rough areas and holding her elbow whenever he thought she might need the help. It was unnecessary, but she didn't mind. Some kinds of protection were pleasant, especially when they involved bodily contact.

As for the cold, the steady climb was making her perspire, not freeze. Without making it obvious, Callie slowly opened the zipper of the down coat Mike had insisted she wear. Honestly, the man had a cold fetish that wouldn't quit. In addition to the coat, she also wore a heavy sweatshirt, which would have been more than enough to keep her warm.

If he ever got past his aversion to marriage and fatherhood, he'd probably be overprotective of their kids, as well. The thought made her smile.

"Let's eat lunch over there," Mike said an hour later, pointing to a place where the glacier had buckled, raising a high block with pinnacles and spires like a fairy-tale castle. They'd be able to eat in the shadow, away from the sun's reflected glare. And it would be more private, though so far they'd seen only a few people in the distance.

"Looks good," she agreed, her voice breathless with the unaccustomed effort.

Mike cast a sideways glance at Callie, trying to tell if she was limping, or if her uneven gait was due to the rugged surface of the ice. She was so obstinate, she'd keep climbing with a broken leg.

Ha, and she called him stubborn. Between the two of them, she had the corner on that particular trait.

"We can't get to the top," he murmured, catching her arm. "It's too far and we don't have the right climbing equipment. We should start back after eating."

"Uh-huh."

Her cheeks were flushed with pink and he frowned. "Hey, your coat is open."

"Yup."

He tugged her to a stop. "Callie, hypothermia isn't a joke."

"Mike, I'm sweating. I grew up in rainy Washington, not the tropics. You have me dressed for a trip to Mount Everest in subzero weather. The sun is shining, it's barely freezing and I'm miserable." She shrugged out of the jacket and thrust it in his arms. "You wanted to carry all our stuff, so carry this."

He scowled...mostly because she was right. He'd chosen to wear just a flannel shirt and vest himself, arguing it was different for Callie because she wasn't used to the cold weather.

She started off again without him and he stood for a minute, admiring her bottom. What Callie lacked in height, she made up for in great curves.

Mike grimaced. He didn't know what to think. They'd almost kissed that morning in the kitchen. Callie had wanted to; he'd seen it in her eyes. But she'd skittered away and the moment was lost.

Just as well.

He'd chosen the glacier for an outing, because it was tough to get into trouble on a giant chunk of ice. The atmosphere simply wasn't conducive to seduction.

So it was safe. He could kiss Callie and not worry about things getting out of control. And he *had* to kiss her again, just to satisfy his curiosity—sort of like a scientific study, or a quality comparison when Triple M was buying a new plane. Otherwise it would drive him out of his mind, wondering which kiss was the best—the one from his fantasy lady, or Callie's.

Liar.

Okay. So he wanted to kiss Callie because he just...*wanted* to. He didn't need any comparison to know that Callie was the hottest thing he'd ever held in his arms, though it seemed strange when she was also the sweetest, most tenderhearted person he knew.

In fact, the whole idea of making love to Callie bordered on irreverent. Not that he didn't want to, but the memory of her wearing a choir robe and playing the organ was a terrific deterrent. Though he had to admit the outrageous outfits she'd worn since arriving had gone a long ways toward erasing that particular memory.

Sighing, Mike trudged after Callie and tossed her the coat. "At least sit on this while we're eating. Your bottom will freeze."

"My bottom isn't any of your business."

He lifted his eyebrows and waggled them at her. "Honey, your fanny is definitely my business."

"Hey, I'm free and single—what I sit on is my own concern." Nevertheless, she dropped the coat onto the thermal blanket he was spreading out and sank down with an unconscious sigh of relief.

From the corner of his eye Mike saw her rubbing the muscles in her thigh and winced. He'd set too fast a pace for their climb, as though walking could take care of the heady rush he felt whenever she smiled at him.

This was *Callie*, yet his body kept acting like she'd done a private striptease. Kissing her again would the nuttiest thing he'd ever done, because if things got any warmer between them, it would complicate things something awful. And they were already pretty complicated.

"I…uh…" He cleared his throat. "I hope you like deli sandwiches. I picked them up when we stopped in Kachelak. You have a choice of turkey or turkey."

"In that case I'll take turkey." Callie removed her gloves and took the offered sandwich. "But I could have made us a lunch."

"Cook?" He dramatically clasped his hand to his chest. "You?"

"Is that supposed to mean something, or are you just being obnoxious?" She unwrapped the sandwich and chomped down on the crusty bread. A bit of mayonnaise clung to the corner of her mouth and she swiped it with the tip of her tongue.

A surge of heat hit Mike's groin and he deliberately focused his eyes on a point a half mile in the distance. "I was being obnoxious," he agreed. "Anyway, you said you didn't want to waste time cooking while you were here. Right?"

Callie wrinkled her nose. Trust Mike to remember every little thing she'd said. "I still could have made us lunch. It's not that big a deal."

"Yeah, but this way you didn't have to." He smiled and she forgave him for everything. At least she forgave him for making her wear a goose down coat when a sweatshirt would have been enough.

She poured coffee from the thermos, and Mike took a big gulp from the steaming cup, then held it out. Callie shook her head—she wasn't as eager to consume any liquid. Men had a distinct advantage when there weren't any public bathrooms in sight.

On the other hand, the scenery was finer than the most expensive restaurant, including Seattle's spectacular Space Needle. As far as the eye could see lay a world of glistening blues, from the sapphire sky to the frozen blue of the glacier.

"Why isn't it whiter?" she asked after a moment, her forehead creased in concentration.

Mike leaned back lazily, munching on one of the pickles that had come with their sandwiches. "I don't know. It has something to do with light absorption."

It made sense to Callie. A prism didn't have any color, either, but it splintered light into a rainbow. She glanced at Mike, who had finished his sandwich and was lying back, fully relaxed despite their chilly surroundings. As a matter of fact, he looked too comfortable.

She nudged him with her foot. "I know we're sitting on ice, but the ground doesn't feel that cold."

He nodded. "It's the thermal blanket. I always carry them with me—they were invented to use in space, but they work down here, too. The shiny side reflects every scrap of heat. They're great in survival situations."

Curious, Callie examined the unusual blanket—black on one side and shiny silver on the other. It was probably like the one she carried in her car's emergency kit, though she'd never had a reason to unwrap it.

"I guess you have to think more about survival up here," she murmured.

"All the time."

Mike opened his eyes a crack and glanced at Callie. Her face was somber, and he wondered if she was starting to understand about life in Alaska. Alaska was a great state, but it had some challenges that couldn't be ignored. Such as subzero storms. Or animals that could kill you with a single swipe of their paw. And only five hours of daylight in the winter. If Callie really understood all that, she'd never stay.

Suddenly the bottom of his stomach didn't feel so great, though he should have been pleased. Callie didn't belong in Alaska, no matter what Ross and Donovan said.

Splinters of cold fell on his face, and his eyes shot open. Callie was leaning over him, laughing as she crumbled a handful of surface snow in her hand.

"You have no respect, woman," he growled.

"I forgot—you're practicing your caveman routine

today, so you demand respect. Only, I didn't know cavemen wanted respect—just a club, a haunch of meat and a woman. Or do you need a harem?"

She looked so alive, filled with laughter and fun. Slowly he touched her lips. Not cold, despite the chilly air and the shadow under which they sat, but warm and supple.

"No answer?"

"One at a time is fine by me."

"I see." She laughed again. "You're like a sailor, then, with a woman in every town and borough. That could get confusing, keeping it all straight."

"I don't have anything of the kind."

Callie put her arm across his chest, her hip snuggled up next to his. For a fraction of a second he couldn't move, the only part of his body that functioned being an inconveniently *demanding* part. Thank goodness for a sturdy pair of underwear and jeans.

"I don't know… The girls used to call you Stud Fitzpatrick—or did you know that?" she asked teasingly. "Someone called Stud Fitzpatrick must have worn out several 'little black books.'"

Mike smiled ruefully. In his wildest imagination, he wouldn't have thought Callie knew his high school nickname. As a teenager he'd strutted over that moniker; now it sounded foolish.

"I haven't been Stud Fitzpatrick for a long time," he murmured, brushing his fingers over her cheeks and easing them through the thick length of her hair. Callie's eyes widened as though startled.

"You… Maybe we should start back…for Kachelak."

Interesting.

Since she'd arrived in Alaska, Callie had been relatively unflappable. Confident and audacious, right down to her tight little tube top. It was nice to know he could send a flicker of uncertainty through her—she'd certainly sent a few flickers through him... amongst other responses.

"We have plenty of time."

"But I should do some work...at least take the messages off the machine."

"Naw. You're taking the day off."

Callie would have pulled away, but the look in Mike's eyes was too tempting. Heat and need and laughter, all rolled into one. She could almost swear this was what he'd had in mind the whole time.

"I thought you were worried about the cold."

"Not if I'm on the bottom."

"What do you—"

The startled question strangled in Callie's throat as Mike lifted her over him, his strength never more evident than in the easy movement. The confident grin should have warned her, but she didn't know what to expect anymore from Michael Fitzpatrick.

Callie controlled her breathing with an effort. "Mike, what are you doing?"

"I'm still curious."

He settled her more squarely over him and a piercing ache swept through her abdomen. "A-about what?"

"About kissing you."

"Oh." Callie would have kicked herself for such an inane response, only, her body had turned into syrup. There wasn't enough strength in her to do anything except rest her fingers over the muscular pads on Mike's chest and count the heavy beating of his heart.

"Two old friends should be able to kiss each other, don't you think?" he asked, his hands sliding over the curves of her hips and cupping her bottom.

Mercy. Callie gulped and wondered if the air was thinner on a glacier. It could be the only explanation for the way her head kept spinning, especially when she knew she had to prevent things from going too far.

Remember the last time. He was upset, really upset about kissing you. It was too soon. Mike would just flip out about getting hot and heavy on a glacier, and she'd keep losing ground.

"I thought we were pretending to be strangers."

"Right...except it wasn't working. You were right about that."

It was hard to think, but Callie was practically certain she'd never said it wouldn't work. Maybe she'd thought it wouldn't work, but that was a whole lot different.

"I didn't say any such thing."

He shrugged. "It doesn't matter. I'd want to kiss you, even if we were strangers. I might have even done it quicker than this."

Callie frowned. That didn't sound good. It had to be the "preacher's daughter" thing again—it was the only reason Mike would kiss a stranger faster than he'd kiss her. At least...she thought it was the problem. Her mind wasn't working too well with his hands tripping the light fantastic all over her body.

"Mike...oh...*hell.*"

She didn't care anymore.

Not with his mouth, open and hot, devouring her with a desperate hunger.

Callie gave up, a moan rising deep from her throat and getting lost in the velvet exploration of his tongue sliding between her teeth. She kissed him back, at the same time tugging his shirt open. He wasn't the only one who wanted to explore.

Without thought she straddled his hips, trembling from the throbbing, hungry sensations deep within. Nothing seemed important but imprinting herself with his strength and masculine heat.

"Yes, Callie."

Mike would have laughed with delight if he'd been capable. Kissing Callie was like uncorking a bottle of champagne, filled with flavor and bubbles and sparkle.

No, better, he thought.

No more fantasy kisses. For the rest of his life he'd compare everything to Callie. It might be worse, knowing exactly how much he'd missed...but it was the price he'd pay for having her this moment.

She drew back minutely and the tip of her tongue traced his lips. "Do you like that?" Callie whispered.

"Yes. Come closer and I'll like it better."

A husky laugh danced through her, but she didn't obey, drifting down his body instead. She tugged gently at the hair on his chest, then traced his nipples, teasing them as he'd teased her, smiling as his muscles clenched.

Though burning, Mike watched through half-closed eyes. Callie knew exactly what she was doing to him, and she reveled in the feminine power she wielded. Yet that power was sweetly bewitching, because she only used it for his pleasure. The knowledge alone heightened his desire.

The scented curtain of her hair fell around them, glowing warmth in the middle of unbroken white as she found his mouth again. He wrapped one hand in the silken wealth and eased under the hem of her sweatshirt with the other.

"My turn," he murmured, tracing a line up her back, reveling in the silken resilience of her skin.

Callie sucked in her breath as Mike released the clasp of her bra. Her breasts swelled, and a second later her nipples crinkled tight and hard, first from the chill contact of his fingers, then with desire.

Slowly, with teasing torture, Mike lifted her above him. He pulled her higher until his mouth could reach each rosy crest in turn, drawing lightly, then strongly, making her squirm with frantic need.

She wanted to touch him, too, and she pleaded in meaningless words and movements, finally caressing him with the only part of her she could...her legs finding his hips, then brushing the swollen bulge between.

"No." Mike's voice, harsh and guttural, tore through Callie. The world turned upside down as he twisted with her in his arms. His fingers clamped her shoulders, and she feared he would stop. Then his gaze fastened on her breasts, taut and bare, her sweatshirt pushed high above them.

Was he comparing them to the other women he must have known? For an instant she was more vulnerable and exposed than she'd ever felt before, and she tried to cover herself.

"No...Callie. You're beautiful," Mike whispered. His hands eased down, the calloused surface of his thumbs brushing across the rosy peaks. His breath warmed and tantalized, mixing with the chill glacier air as he tasted her.

She moaned and arched. Would it ever be enough? Could even Mike ease this terrible, wonderful hurting? She didn't know, because there had never been anyone who made her feel a fraction of the response he provoked so easily.

Mike suckled Callie, filling his mouth with her generous warmth, lost to the violent demand beating inside his body. All the good sense in the world didn't count for anything.

It was only when he tried to unbuckle Callie's belt and her fingers tangled with his, trying to help, that a shred of sanity returned.

Glacier.

You damned *fool.*

Stop. You can't make love to Callie like this, not in front of the whole world.

Groaning, his body screaming for release, Mike rolled over and hit his fist into the ice. The pain was welcome, shooting up his arm and distracting him fractionally from the deeper torture.

"*Mike?*"

"Don't touch me!"

Shocked, Callie jerked away, tears burning in her eyes. It had happened again. Mike had been ready to make love, and he'd stopped. All the hopes and dreams she'd spun coming to Alaska seemed to crumble with the realization.

Mike would never accept her as a woman.

She would always be something less, no matter how hard she tried.

"Fine, have it your way. It was just a friendly, platonic kiss. Why would I think you wanted more?" Callie sat up, turning and fastened her bra. She wouldn't give Mike the satisfaction of seeing her cry. At least she had her dignity, though that was battered, as well.

"Callie, please...it isn't you."

She scooted away, clear off the thermal blanket, and yanked her sweatshirt down. The ice was cold on her bottom, but it was nothing to the ice crystallizing inside her chest.

"Damnation, we're out in the middle of a glacier," Mike snapped. "Anybody could see us."

Callie looked around. On one side sat the ice formation that shaded them, and everywhere else it was limitless white—not even showing distant specks that could be other sightseers.

"Oh, right," she muttered sarcastically. "We're right in the middle of rush-hour traffic, sitting here— we're in real danger of being interrupted."

Grabbing the despised down coat, Callie started walking in the direction they'd come from.

She didn't want to talk anymore. For that matter, she didn't even want to look at Mike. And if he had any sense, he'd just leave her alone.

Chapter Nine

His body groaning in protest, Mike got up and followed Callie. Catching her wrist, he pulled her to stop...and almost wished he hadn't.

The joy and laughter so much a part of her face was gone, her green eyes dark with pain. He'd never intended to hurt Callie; she'd been hurt enough. If fate had been kinder, she would have been married a long time ago, with the houseful of children she'd always wanted.

"Callie, I shouldn't have started anything. I just thought it was safe out here."

"Safe?"

"You know...safe from things getting out of control."

Her lips hardened into a straight line and anger replaced the hurt in her eyes. "Thank goodness you stayed safe. I mean, it would have been really awful making love to me."

"That's not what I meant."

"No? Don't tell me..." Callie pressed her hand over her heart in pretend shock. "You're a virgin, and you've been saving yourself for marriage."

"I'm not a virgin."

"Well, then, it must be me."

"It's not like that. You're gorgeous, you're just..."

"The preacher's daughter." Her voice was flat, not even questioning. And even though Mike suspected it was a mistake, he could only agree.

"Honey, that's who you are."

"If I was Mary Jo Lowry, you would have had sex with me. Heck, you would have had sex in the plane, or in the truck for that matter."

Mary Jo? Mike thought back frantically, finally remembering the woman Callie meant. "Mary Jo Lowry?" he repeated incredulously. "Mary Jo was going steady with the football team. She slept with anything wearing pants. You're not like that."

"I'm a woman, but that seems to have escaped your notice." Callie spun on her heel and continued marching down the hill.

Cursing beneath his breath, Mike went back to gather the remnants of their picnic.

Not notice Callie was a woman?

Did she think he was blind?

He settled the pack on his shoulders and looked down the glacier. In the few short minutes it had taken to stuff everything into the backpack, she'd already gained a quarter-mile lead.

Fear replaced other emotions as Mike remembered her tumble earlier in the day. She was so upset, she wouldn't look for crevasses, or any of the hidden dangers of the glacier.

He put his hands to his mouth and shouted. "Callie!

Stop right now.'' Sound echoed across the ice, but she didn't even hesitate. Mike finally stopped wasting his breath and hurried after her.

For such a small woman, she had an amazing ability to move quickly. There was little he could do except keep his eyes focused on her and pray she wouldn't do something stupid.

Like trusting you?

Again?

You're an idiot. Do you know that?

His conscience wasn't any help under the circumstances. It jeered sarcastic reproofs with every step. At the same time, he couldn't help questioning why Callie had come to Alaska in the first place.

Shreds of information filtered through his churning thoughts. Callie, with her own business—apparently a successful one, if her ability in their own office was any indication. Strong, successful, certain of herself... Why would she come to Alaska for an entire summer?

His stride lengthened.

Answers. He wanted answers, and Callie saying she wanted a vacation wouldn't cut it this time.

He caught up near the mouth of the glaciers. The deep ravines and cracks through the ice were singing with melting water, rushing to freedom.

"Damn it, Callie Webster. Talk to me."

"We have nothing to discuss."

"You were willing to make love with me up there...you're furious because I stopped. What the hell is going on?"

She planted her hands on her hips and glared. "*Damn? Hell?* Is that the proper language to use around a 'preacher's daughter'? Because that's all I am, right?"

Mike growled another, more vicious curse. "Why did you come up here, Callie? The truth this time."

An array of emotions crossed her face. Rage, doubt, defiance…and finally disdain. "All right, I came to Alaska to marry you. Funny, isn't it?"

His jaw dropped, though the suspicion must have been coiling through his subconscious for a long while. "You came to—"

"Catch you. Make you fall in love with me. Do I have to spell it out? You're a big dumb jerk, but I thought I was in love. So go ahead and laugh."

Love. That word had always scared him. Love meant forever, and he didn't want forever. It meant all the ties and boundaries, and sameness of life in every little town in America.

Callie smiled, a hard, clear smile. "Don't look so worried, Mike. I have standards, too. I wouldn't marry you now if you were the last man on earth."

"Why, because I respected you up there?"

"It's not respect," she snapped. "It's a whole way of looking at me. I'm a preacher's daughter, but that's only a tiny part of who I am."

Mike set his jaw. "I know that."

"Do you? I'm a woman, with the same feelings and needs as any other woman. And if you won't treat me that way, I'll find somebody who will."

"I didn't mean—"

"And if you were half the man I thought you were, you would have seen it a long time ago," she continued without drawing breath. "Then I wouldn't have needed to come up here and make a fool of myself."

"You didn't make a fool of yourself."

"No? Do the calculation again."

He took a deep breath, trying to sort his jumbled thoughts. "I care about you."

"Do you love me?" Callie asked grimly.

Mike opened his mouth, but the words got stuck in his throat. Love? He didn't know what love meant, and he sure didn't know if he loved her. *Cared,* yes. Damnation, he thought the world of Callie; she was sweet, generous and so special he ached just looking at her.

But love?

"Look," he said desperately. "Maybe we need some time to sort things out."

"We've had a long time, Mike. More than thirty years. I hardly think more time is going to change anything."

Callie's jaw hurt from the effort she was making not to scream or do anything else to humiliate herself. The world wouldn't end if Mike didn't love her, and it certainly wouldn't come crashing to a halt because he'd refused to make love to her on a glacier, or anywhere else.

But she couldn't fight it any longer.

She'd taken the risk, gambling that Mike would be able to see past their childhood and realize she had a lot to offer him. And she'd lost. No matter what, she didn't want to spend her life trapped by that label. *Preacher's daughter.* She'd read enough about men to know they didn't stop when things had gone so far.

Yet, it wasn't only the way he'd broken things off. Mike had obviously never even considered being in love with her, and that hurt most of all. He was so darned stubborn about his freedom, he might never discover how he really felt.

She crossed her arms over her stomach and looked

around. Beauty surrounded them, but it didn't seem beautiful anymore. "I want to get out of here," she whispered.

Mike reached out as if to touch her and she flinched. His arm dropped and he thrust his hands into his pockets. "Sure. It's about a mile to the truck. We can be home in a couple of hours."

In silence they made their way to the Dodge Dakota. It was all Callie could manage, not to fly apart completely.

Home?

What a joke. Mike's house wasn't a home; it was just a big empty building he rattled around in. She'd been so hopeful when she'd seen the house—it was such a perfect place to raise kids, and he must have known it was too large and impractical for a single person.

Another two hours, she told herself. Then she'd pack her bags and move to Donovan's place. It would be a lot better than staying with Mike and the constant reminder that life didn't always work out according to plan.

When they stopped by the house, she opened the vehicle door and slid out in a single, silent motion.

"Callie...wait. We have to talk."

"We already talked. I have to make a phone call," she muttered.

Mike watched Callie disappear up the stairs and swore under his breath. There were about a hundred ways he could have handled that scene on the glacier. *Better* ways. He'd always considered himself a tactful person, but his brain had overloaded between her astonishing announcement and the hard flush of passion still demanding release.

Things were quiet for a while, then he heard her moving around her room, accompanied by a lot of bumping and thumping. He sighed; he wouldn't blame Callie if she trashed the place. In fact, he'd feel a lot better if she broke something.

Precisely twenty-five minutes later Callie came walking down the staircase with her suitcases, a grim expression on her face. Unaccustomed panic hit Mike and he jumped to his feet, knocking the chair over in his haste.

"Callie, where are you going?"

"That's none of your business."

She shouldered past him and stomped out to the truck Ross had loaned her. The suitcases landed carelessly in the back and she fished the keys from her purse.

"Wait a minute." His mind was spinning with possibilities, the worst being that Callie intended to go back to Washington. He didn't want that, at least not until they'd sorted things out. "You can't...go home."

"Please." She rolled her eyes in disgust. "Don't worry. I'll stay and keep the office running for the summer. I'm just moving in with Donovan."

Mike gulped, realizing there were worse possibilities than Callie returning to Washington.

I'm a woman, with the same feelings and needs as any other woman. And if you won't treat me that way, I'll find somebody who will.

"You can't do that," he said harshly.

"Watch me."

"For God's sake," he snarled. "Be reasonable. You surprised me and I didn't handle it well. I'm sorry."

"It doesn't matter."

Hell.

Mike tightened his hand. It throbbed and he glanced at his fist with surprise—the skin was crisscrossed with small abrasions, seeping blood. How did that happen?

The ice.

Oh, yeah, he'd hit his hand on the ice, trying to get some control over his body—some help *that* had been.

"Look," he said, trying to sound calm and reasonable. "I don't understand.... You were engaged to be married. How could you have feelings for me?"

Her face shadowed. "I loved Keith. He was good and kind and decent. We would have had a happy marriage. You were just this stupid infatuation. It's time I got it out of my system. So thank you very much for the help."

"Infatuation?" he asked incredulously.

Callie tightened her lips. Her pride had been speaking, not her heart. In fact, her pride had started the whole argument. There had to be a way to get out of this mess without shredding what remained of her self-respect.

"There isn't any point in discussing this. Get out of my way."

"You're not moving in with Donovan!"

She smiled sweetly...showing her teeth. "Do me a favor—go jump off a glacier. You don't have any say in this."

"The hell I don't." Mike reached into the pickup bed for her suitcases, and Callie gave him a shove. It was like pushing on a rock. "You're not doing something you'll regret," he snapped.

"It's too late—I already regret ever meeting you." She planted her hands on her hips. "Now leave my stuff alone."

"No." He carried her luggage toward the house and she glared.

"Fine. I'll sleep in the nude."

Callie had reached the driver's side when Mike grabbed her by the waist and whirled her around. "I said you're not going to Donovan's." A muscle twitched in his jaw and he looked ready to explode.

"Leave me alone, Mike. I've taken a number of self-defense classes, and I know where a man is particularly vulnerable." She gave him a comprehensive examination from head to toe. "And as much as I hate to bolster your ego any further, you do provide a generous target."

Mike's eyes widened, then narrowed to mere slits. "You wouldn't."

"How bad do you want to find out?"

He swore—a short, precise and extremely earthy expletive—and released her.

"Precisely."

Callie got into the truck and drove out of the driveway. In the rearview mirror she saw Mike stomping around the side of his house. Probably to chop more wood. She'd never seen anyone chop so much wood.

Well, fine.

It wasn't her concern anymore.

But she was shaking, and when she got to a good spot on the road, she pulled off and sat for a long time.

"I hate him," she whispered finally, unable to even cry.

If anything else happened between her and Mike, he'd have to be the one doing the chasing. She was finished with that routine. If the idiot didn't know what he was missing, then she wasn't going to beat herself senseless trying to make him understand.

* * *

The next day Callie got to the office at 6:00 a.m., her eyes gritty from lack of sleep.

"Ohmigod, I didn't know the sun rose this early," Donovan groaned as he followed her inside. "Are you sure you don't want the day off?"

Faint humor curved her lips. Were all men this bad in the morning, or just the ones who lived in Alaska? Not that she should complain—Donovan had been so sweet, getting her things from Mike's house and setting her up in a spare bedroom.

"You could have stayed in bed," she murmured. "I'm a big girl—I don't need baby-sitting."

Donovan sank onto one of the low file cabinets and shook his head. "Nope. If Mike shows up, I want to punch his lights out."

"So do I," Ross said, walking through the door.

Callie shook her head. "What are you doing here? It must have been after midnight when you got in from California."

"Actually it was after 2:00 a.m." He shrugged. "And I'm here to offer moral support."

"How do you...?" Her voice trailed off as he gave her one of his kind smiles.

"Donovan told me. I can't believe Mike is acting this way. For a bright guy, he's been pretty stupid."

"Stupid" was right, but Callie didn't know what to do about it. Maybe things weren't fixable between them. She'd come to Alaska all determined and certain of what she wanted, and now she was having as many doubts as Mike.

"I have a plan—we'll hold him down while Callie kicks him," Donovan said, his eyes closed as he rested his head against the wall. "Then we get our turn. How about it, Callie?"

Ross rubbed his hands together. "Sounds good to me."

Donovan had already offered to punch Mike's lights out about ten times, and while the idea appealed to her, she wasn't *that* mad at him.

In all honesty, she'd overreacted. But the way he'd ended their last two kisses seemed ominous. And she couldn't forget the kiss on the night she'd arrived...when he'd fallen asleep.

Hardly something to make a woman feel desirable. Until now she'd been able to dismiss it because Mike had been tired and a little drunk.

Not that drunk.

No, Mike had only drunk a small amount of Scotch, and it wasn't enough to explain him falling asleep in the middle of a passionate, all-out, body-parts-included kiss.

"How about it, Callie? You get first dibs on damaging Mike, then we'll beat the hell out him."

"That just macho garbage. I have a much better idea," Callie said. She pointed at Donovan and grinned. "Don't tell him we're not sleeping together."

The other man grinned back. "Good idea... Let's torture him for a while. Of course, if you change your mind about that 'sleeping with me' part, I'll be happy to oblige."

It was the first time since she'd arrived at his place—white-faced and hardly able to talk—that Donovan had made one of his teasing remarks, and she laughed.

"I'll keep that in mind."

Feeling better, Callie filled the office coffeepot with

water. She added extra grounds to the filter and flipped the switch. After a few minutes Ross and Donovan migrated out to the hangar, appearing occasionally to check on her, sheepish expressions on their faces.

What did they think, she'd slit her wrists?

Not likely. Self-annihilation was messy and uncomfortable. Beating up Mike had more appeal, but she wasn't planning to do that, either. Actually, making love with Mike had the most appeal, except she wasn't getting into another clinch with Michael Fitzpatrick unless she had a ring on her finger and a marriage certificate on the dresser. It wasn't worth the heartache.

Drat.

Callie opened and slammed a few drawers for the mere pleasure of hearing the loud crack.

All thoughts led back to Mike, even after what he'd done...or rather, what he *hadn't* done. She'd have to do some long hard thinking before she married him— no way was she going to spend her life trapped in someone else's idea of how she should act.

The minor physical violence helped calm her nerves, and she settled down to work.

Several hours later Mike drove up outside and she put her head down, staring at the computer like it was the most important thing she'd ever seen.

"Callie?"

"What?"

"Please look at me. I brought something for you."

Keeping her lips in a straight line, she swiveled in the chair. Mike stood near the desk holding a bouquet of irises. In addition to jeans, he wore a white shirt and tie, and his hair was neatly combed. He looked just like a kid, coming to apologize...only, no kid had ever been so overwhelmingly virile. The white shirt only emphasized his wide shoulders, and the worn jeans showed his flat stomach and muscular legs to great advantage.

Phew.

She resisted the urge to fan herself. Men like that were dangerous; they could give a woman amnesia about all kinds of rotten, frustrating moments. And she needed her wits to keep from doing something more foolish than she'd already done...like confessing she loved him.

Callie shuddered and shoved a pencil in the drawer, slamming it again.

"Callie..." Mike cleared his throat and shifted from one foot to the other, apparently at a loss for words.

Huh, did he think flowers would turn her into sloppy sentimental goo? Not a chance.

On closer examination she could see his right eye was puffy and beginning to turn black. A Band-Aid adorned the area above his eyebrow and a second one covered the back of his hand.

Uh-oh.

Somebody had gotten physical.

"Donovan?" she called.

Donovan appeared at the door and gave her a cheeky grin. "Yes, sweetheart?"

Callie pointed to Mike. "Did you do that?" she asked sternly.

"Certainly not. I know how much you hate that macho garbage." He winked and disappeared again.

Mike gritted his teeth to keep from demanding what had happened between Callie and the other man. The jealousy he'd felt before was nothing to what he felt knowing she'd moved in with Donovan.

"So, how did you get the shiner?" she asked, sounding like she didn't care one way or the other.

"It's nothing. I...fell."

A disgusted sound came from her throat. "Don't tell me you got drunk."

"No. Look, I'm sorry, Callie." He put the irises on the desk and tried to catch her eyes. "Would you please talk to me?"

"We have nothing to discuss."

"You said you loved me."

"I don't care what I said," she interjected hastily.

This wasn't hopeful, but he hadn't expected things to be easy. Of course, he shouldn't have brought up the *L* word, especially when he didn't know what to say about it in the first place.

"Uh...I brought flowers...your favorite."

Callie slapped a file down on the desk and glared. "How would you know I like irises? Did you call Elaine?"

"I remembered—you always loved them when we were kids."

"Ha." She obviously didn't believe him, and Mike couldn't really blame her. Callie had played a part in every important event of his childhood, and yet he'd virtually ignored her since moving from Crockett.

"And I've got something else you like," he said quickly. "Just a minute. I'll get it."

He walked outside and picked up an animal carrier. A hiss and growl came from the contents and he hesitated; maybe this wasn't such a great idea, but Callie was waiting and he'd already opened his big mouth.

Mike returned to the office and carefully closed the door. "Here. It's something to help with those mice in the storeroom. Only, be careful. I don't think he's too sociable.''

Callie wasn't ready to forgive Mike, but she smiled at the heavily whiskered cat poking its paw at her through the narrow openings in the carrier. Cats were some of her favorite people.

''Hello, beauty. Do you want out?''

''I mean it,'' Mike said quickly. ''He's kind of unsettled and you don't want to get scratched.''

Ignoring the warning, she undid the carrier. A large black cat leapt out and started preening itself on her lap. She rubbed the feline's neck and he purred in a loud rumble, arching himself against her.

''I'll be damned. He's a changeling.''

Mike stared at the affectionate cat and Callie suppressed a giggle, suddenly suspecting where the black eye and scratches had come from.

''What's his name?'' she asked.

''Uh...Precious, if you can believe it. But he deserves a few less civilized names,'' Mike said darkly. ''Some friends have been trying to find a home for this guy, and now I know why. Of course, at the time they said he was just shy and leery of the carrier.''

She rubbed the whiskered face and the purr doubled in volume. ''You just don't know how to talk to cats.''

Mike nodded. He also didn't know how to talk to preacher's daughters who'd turned into sexy bombshells; it wasn't something within his experience. Yet, no matter how much she protested, Callie was still the same girl who'd always been so sweet and fun when they were kids, there was just a new dimension to her. A pretty sensational dimension, and he'd been blind not to see it.

''Callie...please move back to the house.''

The pleasure in her face faded and she lifted her chin. "No way. I'm happy at Donovan's."

He sighed. Apparently even a cat wasn't enough to make her forgive him. Somehow he'd made a terrible mistake, though he wasn't entirely sure what he'd done wrong. He'd stopped in the middle of a kiss, but women were always protesting that men weren't sensitive enough, and all they thought about was sex.

Just then Callie put Precious down on the floor, leaning over to toss a small wad of paper for him to chase. The fabulous view of her bottom made Mike gulp.

Of course, sex was pretty great.

Mike shook his head. Okay, he *was* a sex-minded caveman, but that was beside the point. With any other woman, showing respect would have been a plus—a sensitive, modern man sort of action.

But not to Callie.

His face fell. Callie wasn't like other women. How could he possibly understand her?

And more importantly, how could he get her back?
Get her back?

As in love and marriage?

The room seemed awfully warm all of a sudden and Mike loosened his tie. What a dumb idea, wearing a tie. It was more apt to make Callie laugh than listen.

Damn. Callie might have grown up in Crockett, but she was anything but boring. As a matter of fact, she was bright, sassy, sexy and utterly desirable. A man would be damned lucky to have her for a wife.

Another man's wife...unless he got her to forgive him.

Mike groaned. He might have lost the best thing that had ever happened to him.

Chapter Ten

Six mornings later Mike drove into the airfield. He parked the Dakota and rubbed his throbbing temples. So far, all his efforts to make peace with Callie had been spectacularly unsuccessful.

"This is getting ridiculous," he muttered.

He lifted a sixth bouquet of irises from the seat beside him and trudged into the office. Precious lounged in feline splendor on the desk, cleaning his whiskers. The end of his tail twitched when Mike put the flowers next to him, and he opened his mouth in a soundless hiss.

"The same back, you little monster." Mike's relations with Precious hadn't improved over the past week, either.

"Rrowrrr."

Callie appeared from the storeroom, lugging a case of motor oil, and he grabbed it from her. "That's too heavy—why didn't you ask one of us to get it?"

She blew a damp strand of hair from her forehead

and gave him one of her drop-dead looks. "I don't need your help."

"Damn it." Mike lugged the oil to the hangar and stomped back inside. "You are so stubborn. Could we please declare a truce and talk this out?"

Callie put her chin up, determined not to back down. Okay, it was mostly wounded pride that wouldn't let her talk to Mike, but if he said he "cared" about her one more time, she'd belt him herself.

Cared?

Yuck. "Caring" was nice and sweet and it didn't have any passion in it. The man set her on fire. She didn't want *caring,* she wanted mad, passionate love. And she wanted a husband and father of her children.

Even if he hadn't admitted it, she suspected Mike loved her. But *who* did he want? The flirt in a tube top and jeans? Or the woman who wanted to be sexy, as well as being a good cook and mother? Could she hide half of her identity forever, just to be with the man she loved? It was a tough question, and she couldn't talk to him until she figured it out for herself.

Lifting one eyebrow, she shrugged. "Talk about what?"

"Sheesh, you're stubborn." He threw his hands up and stomped out of the room.

Callie stroked the velvet petals of the irises he'd left on her desk. She was tempted to toss them in the garbage, but they were too pretty to destroy.

Sighing, she returned to the storeroom, this time with Precious following her. To date he'd generously presented fourteen trophies for her inspection—eleven mice, two rats and something that looked like a cartoon animal.

Live mice were annoying but cute. Dead ones turned her stomach.

That was the worst part about his diligent hunting...aside from his leaving them on her chair. She'd sprayed and disinfected the chair so many times the office smelled like a hospital.

"You should try to get along with Mike," Callie advised the black feline, who was busily sniffing a stack of boxes in the corner. "After I leave, you'll be stuck with him."

Precious let out an eerie cry—either a hunting challenge, or a comment on the company he was expected to keep come wintertime.

"Fine, have it your way."

Callie sat cross-legged on the floor and looked through a box of pictures she'd discovered a few days before. It was pure, weak indulgence. They were mostly of Mike, Ross and Donovan when they'd worked on the Alaska pipeline together, and during the early years when Triple M Transit had been so new.

She'd selected several to be framed and hung in the office—one of their first cargo plane, the three of them grinning ear to ear in front of it—and others that showed the expansion of the company. But it was the photos of Mike she kept poring over.

He'd changed so much, yet he had the same quick smile and adventurous nature she'd first loved about him. Maybe she was being unreasonable, wanting him to see her in a different way. Maybe it was impossible.

"Mrroww?"

Precious bumped his head against her and she stroked his back. "I don't want to be 'innocent' Callie all my life," she whispered. "Expected to act a certain way, and shocking my husband if I wear a slinky dress. I want both.''

''Hey, Callie, talking to yourself?'' Donovan called from the other room.

''No, I'm talking to Precious. He carries on a better conversation than most men.''

''Ouch...I guess Mike has been in for his daily dose of groveling.''

Callie put the photos back in the box and got up, dusting her jeans. ''Been and gone.''

''You'll have to talk to him sometime.''

She resisted making a biting retort. Mike's partners had been kind and supportive, but they were also his friends. They wanted the situation resolved, almost as much as she did.

''Bet you wish I never came to Alaska,'' she said.

''Nope.'' Donovan was awkwardly putting the irises into an old coffee can and she took over, to his obvious relief. ''Hell, we'd sink without you at this point, and I think Curdgeon Post would skin our hides. He's pretty fond of you.''

''I like Curdgeon. He talks rough, but inside he's a romantic.''

Donovan laughed. ''Have it your way. Actually, Ross and I think you should become a partner in the company. That way you can't leave.''

''I'll bet Mike loves that idea,'' Callie said dryly.

''He isn't against it.''

Startled, her gaze flew to Donovan to see how serious he might be. ''You're kidding.''

''Nope, it was the first time in over a week that he *hasn't* bitten our heads off.''

Callie filled the can with water, her forehead creased in thought. She didn't care about becoming a partner, but the fact that Mike didn't oppose the idea might mean he didn't want her to leave.

Hope sprang eternal, and every day she fell deeper in love with Mike, no matter how hard she tried not to. What a muddle.

She was right.

Mike was right.

And neither one of them had a solution.

Mike brought his ax down and split the log cleanly in two. He'd only split about a million pieces of wood since Callie had shown up in Kachelak instead of his sister, but he couldn't stand being in the house.

It was too quiet—all he could think about was Callie living at Donovan's place. He didn't think they were sleeping together, but a tiny element of doubt ate at his gut...along with her threat to find someone who would treat her like a woman.

At any rate, he doubted Callie was having any trouble falling asleep—from all the evidence, both Donovan and Ross were keeping her well occupied.

Damnation.

He'd gotten himself into a fine mess.

What he needed was an excuse to drag her home— to *his* home. The house didn't feel right without Callie, though he didn't think she'd buy that reasoning. He wasn't even sure an "I love you" would cut any ice. Their problems went beyond mutual love, though he'd realized she was more important to him than anyone else in the world.

He didn't know when he'd fallen in love with Callie, but it had happened, and now he was just as pathetic as all the other jerks who'd opened their eyes too late to see the truth.

Boring?

Loving Callie was about as boring as a ride down the Colorado River rapids.

The sound of a ringing phone distracted him, and he strode into the house.

"Yes?"

"Hello, Michael. How are you?" The gentle voice of Callie's father turned Mike into stone.

"Er...Reverend Webster. Hello, sir."

"Is Callie there?"

He clenched the receiver and scowled. So, Callie hadn't told her father she was staying with Donovan Masters. It was completely unreasonable, expecting him to lie for her.

"I'm sorry. She's taking a walk." Mike held his breath, expecting fire and brimstone to come flying out of the sky, or at least out of the phone. He'd never been an angel, but he'd never lied to a preacher before, either.

"Well, I hope she's enjoying her vacation. Please have her call when she comes in."

"Sure, first thing."

Mike slammed the phone down and headed for his truck. A part of him was angry, the other part knew he'd found an excuse to insist Callie move back home.

When he reached Donovan's place he slammed on the brakes and jumped out. The evening sun was mellow, highlighting the figure lying in a hammock on the porch.

Callie.

If she'd heard him arrive, she was ignoring him. One slim leg hung over the edge, nudging the floor as she rocked back and forth. The red tube top she'd worn the first day was snug around her breasts, and she lay with one hand on her stomach in complete relaxation.

She was so beautiful Mike paused for a moment, drinking in the sight of her.

"Callie, we have to talk."

Lazily Callie opened her eyes and shrugged. "It's not office hours, I'm on my own time." Her lids closed again and she kept rocking.

"You won't talk to me at the office."

"So? Fire me."

Mike stomped up the stairs and stood over her. His only consolation was finding Callie alone. He'd spent the drive imagining some lurid scenes between her and Donovan.

"Where's Donovan?"

Her shoulders lifted again. "I don't know. We're roomies, not—"

"*Dammit.*" Mike swept Callie from the hammock, cursing a blue streak. "I won't let you sleep with him."

Callie put her palms on his chest and shoved. "I said roomies, not lovers, you dolt."

"You also said you'd find someone to treat you like a woman. I assumed that meant having sex."

"Cripes." She rolled her eyes. "Ross and Donovan are friends. I can't believe how unreasonable you've become—you don't want to have sex with me, but you think everyone else can't keep their hands off."

"I never said I wouldn't have sex with you."

"Fine, remember it your way." She shook his hands away and glared. "What are you doing here?"

Mike recalled his reason for coming and his temper rose again. "Your father called. I had to lie to him, Callie. I said you were taking a walk. You're coming home with me, right now. I refuse to cover for you again.''

"Don't bother. Dad has this wonderful quality called trust. You should try it sometime.''

"Your father wouldn't understand your living with Donovan,'' Mike shouted. "*I* don't understand.''

"That's because you're a stubborn oaf with the sensitivity of brick,'' she shouted back. "It's my life and my choices. My dad wouldn't dream of interfering, but you're acting like a narrow-minded puritan.''

Her accusation stung, mostly because it was true.

"You're a hypocrite,'' she continued. "You think you're so modern—the man who escaped small-town Crockett and made a name for himself. But look around.'' Callie waved her arm, encompassing the lush hemlock forest that crowded the road and spilled into the yard. "You escaped right into the last wilderness frontier.''

"I like Alaska.''

"I like it, too. But this isn't New York, with subways and lights and glamorous models on every corner.''

"Thank goodness,'' Mike murmured.

"But you're only glad about the subways and lights, right? You'd enjoy the glamorous models,'' she said bitterly.

"That's not what I want.''

"Fine. When you figure out what you want, let me know. In the meantime, I want some peace and quiet. Don't bother saying goodbye.'' Callie slid back into the hammock and determinedly closed her eyes. As far as she was concerned, the argument was over.

Let Mike break someone else's heart.

Still, it was hard to resist the way he looked at her,

his brown eyes filled with longing and desire. Yet, he hadn't said he loved her, just demanded she move back to his house so he wouldn't have to "lie" to her father.

Mike moved past her, and it sounded suspiciously like he was going into the house. Okay, fine. Callie crossed her arms and started the motion going on the hammock. Snoopy, suspicious rat. He wouldn't accept her word; he had to find out for himself that she wasn't sharing a bedroom with Donovan.

A few minutes later a loud clunk vibrated through the porch. Twisting around, she saw her suitcases sitting next to Mike's tapping foot. The lacy edge of a bra stuck out from the top of the shoulder bag, which he hadn't even bothered to zip entirely closed.

A wordless growl came from her throat and she kicked the floor hard with her foot, sending the hammock in a wild arc. "We talked about this before. I'm not going anywhere."

"You're going, even if I have to throw you over my shoulder to get you there."

"I will damage you," Callie said distinctly. "You'll sing soprano for a week, and you won't be able to stand straight for a month."

"Callie, be reasonable."

"You don't have any right to make demands. We aren't married, and we aren't about to be."

A gasp was torn from her throat as Mike dumped her from the hammock, right into his arms. He pinned her to one of the posts supporting the porch and glared.

"That's what you think," he said furiously. "You came to Alaska to catch me, and that's what you've done. Are you woman enough to know what to do with me?"

It was a lousy proposal, Callie thought faintly, her heart racing with both anger and excitement. And he was deliberately taunting her with that "woman enough" routine. Did he think she'd fall for that?

"Mike, let me go."

"No, Callie." He groaned and buried his face in her hair, the hard length of his body branding her with heat and urgency. "Please, honey. I've been a fool, I know that. I don't want to spend the rest of my life without you."

Tears stung her eyes and she put her hands on his waist. Mike shuddered with the touch, moving against her in a way that left no doubt of his intent.

But he'd pulled back too many times, leaving her burning and doubting herself. If it happened again she'd never survive—she wasn't sure either of them would.

"Stop it!" Her fierce tone caught his attention and he eased away, his face drawn with pain.

"It can't be too late. Listen to me."

"I have listened. Let me think." Callie retreated to the end of the porch and clasped her arms around her stomach. She shook like an autumn leaf, partly from Mike's touch, and partly from the emotions tearing at her heart.

"Tell me what to do, Callie."

"It's not you."

"You didn't believe me when I said that, and I don't believe it now."

"It *is* me."

Callie drew a shaky breath and looked down the hill, to where Blying Sound and the Gulf of Alaska gleamed in the distance. It was so lovely, and it would be lovely in winter, as well, no matter how much snow fell, or how cold it got.

Free and wild.

She'd looked for freedom in Alaska, but she'd gotten some painful lessons instead. A place didn't guarantee freedom, and sometimes even love wasn't enough to solve the problems between a man and woman.

"All my life I've been this person…this preacher's daughter," she whispered. "I did what everyone expected, and acted just the way a preacher's daughter should act. I love my father and the church, except it's such a tiny part of who I am, and sometimes I felt so trapped."

Mike watched her silently and she dashed a tear from her cheek.

"Then for a little while, I was free. Keith made me laugh, and he loved me so much. Maybe I didn't love him the way he loved me, but I did love him. And it felt so good when we were together."

Callie looked down at the floor, fighting for words to explain everything she'd never said.

"He understood about the church and my father, and I suppose he held back because of it, but he accepted all of me…loved all of me."

A strangled, anguished sound came from Mike's throat and his mouth tightened into a white line.

She swallowed and continued. "When Keith died, it seemed like a punishment for wanting something beyond Crockett. I felt so guilty. Then time passed and I realized it wasn't punishment. It was just an accident. A stupid, senseless accident."

Mike hadn't realized he could hurt this badly— maybe because he'd never loved another person quite so much. And he couldn't do anything to help, only listen.

"So I started my own business and tried to have a life of my own. Except I kept being the preacher's daughter and suffocating on everyone's expectations." Callie rubbed her palms over her jeans and sighed. "I wanted to escape, but I didn't."

"Until now."

She smiled sadly. "That wasn't an escape—I got to Alaska and found Crockett waiting for me. You had the same expectations, the same mental image of who I was, and how I should act. I just changed addresses, that's all."

"It doesn't have to be like this," Mike said urgently. "I was protecting myself. I didn't understand. You can be free here, we can work it out." He took a step forward, but she shook her head.

"I'm scared, Mike. I love you, but I can't live like that anymore."

"You don't have to," he promised softly.

Callie wiped more tears from her cheeks. It all boiled down to courage, and it had taken a lot to come to Alaska in the first place.

"I've loved you all my life. At least I thought it was love," she whispered. "You don't remember, but we even kissed the night you graduated from college."

Shock swept through Mike and he froze. It was Callie, that night. *She* was the fantasy girl he'd dreamt about for years. What a damned fool he'd been, not seeing something so remarkable, right in front of him.

"Think about it." Callie motioned to her red tube top with a funny smile. "I'm still the same person who enjoys baking cakes for the church potluck and teaches

Sunday. And I'm a woman who wears seductive clothing to intrigue the man she loves.''

He rubbed the back of his neck. "I don't understand—I know you're all of that."

She sighed. "I want to be a wife, a mother, a partner...but I don't want you seeing a preacher's daughter in your bed, instead of a lover."

"Believe me, that's not going to happen."

"No? You stopped, Mike—in the plane, on the glacier. You said it the first day. I'm not that kind of woman."

"I won't deny I want to protect you," he murmured, picking his words with care. "But that's natural. I also want you. You have no idea how much I want you."

"Ha." Callie crossed her arms over her stomach and glared. She looked so adorable and sexy, he had to hide a smile. Smiling would be politically unwise at this point. "You want to protect me because you think I'm so innocent and sheltered," she said with disgust.

"Because I care so much," Mike corrected gently. "You don't have any reason to believe me, but it's true. All my life I've avoided marriage and commitment—I thought it was a trap. Then all of a sudden you were here and I wanted you...and I knew if we made love, I wouldn't be able to let go."

She didn't say anything, just looked at him with her beautiful, hurting green eyes.

"I never realized the trap isn't marriage, it's being alone."

Callie bit her lip. Mike still hadn't said he'd loved her. She'd taken this big chance, coming to Alaska to catch the man of her dreams, never realizing there were more things to worry about than a broken heart.

"As for stopping… It only went that far because I wanted you so much." Mike held out his hand, urging her to take it. "Please, sweetheart, take a chance. Trust me one more time. I won't let you down."

Callie looked at Mike. She could love him, and take a risk on building a life together, or she could spend the rest of her life alone.

He knelt on one knee. "I love you, Callie Webster. I'll be the luckiest man in the world if you marry me."

Love.

Finally. Laughing and crying at the same time, Callie threw herself into his arms. "It took you long enough," she said. "Of course I'll marry you."

Chapter Eleven

Mike glanced at Callie sitting next to him in the limousine and grinned.

The wedding would be in Anchorage tomorrow, with his parents and sister and a few friends in attendance. Callie's brothers hadn't been able to come on such short notice, but Reverend Webster had flown in the night before and would perform the ceremony.

Unable to contain himself, Mike leaned over and murmured something in Callie's ear before giving her a hard kiss.

Callie didn't know if her head spun more from Mike's provocative words, or from the kiss. She sat back and touched the expensive diamond ring on her finger. She'd protested, saying she didn't need an engagement ring when they were getting married in a week, but she was secretly thrilled Mike had insisted.

Weddings should be preceded by diamonds and suitors on one knee, with impassioned declarations of love.

"We haven't talked about a honeymoon," Mike said as the Cadillac turned out of the airport. "I thought Paris would be nice. Or maybe the Cayman Islands—some place warm and tropical."

"It's warm today, but hardly tropical," she said dreamily.

"Callie," Mike said, exasperated. "I just asked you about a honeymoon, not the weather. Do you prefer Paris or the Cayman Islands, or someplace else?"

Heat burned in her face and she sneaked a glance at him. "Sorry. Isn't this a bad time to leave? Triple M does the majority of its business during the summer."

Mike stroked her cheek with the back of his hand. "I think we're more important than the company. Donovan and Ross said they'd cover for us. Anyway, we'll do the same when they get married."

She laughed. "They're more likely to need wheelchairs and geriatric vitamin pills before they tie the knot."

Mike smiled and lifted Callie to his lap, loving the way her breath caught in her throat. She always responded when he touched her. Waiting to make love had been the hardest thing he'd ever done, but it was what she'd wanted.

"Now I know why you ordered the limousine," she whispered between kisses.

"Mmm…yes. It leaves my hands free for more important things." He cupped her breast and rubbed his thumb across a nipple, already hardening against the softness of her silk blouse. "One more night," he murmured.

One more night…

The words echoed in Callie's mind and she moaned.

Why had she insisted on that "no sex until we get married" routine? She must have been insane.

"Mr. Fitzpatrick?" The voice of the limo driver came through the intercom and they both jerked upright. "We'll be at the hotel in a couple of minutes."

Callie hastily tucked her blouse into the waistband of her skirt and smoothed her hair. She might want to escape the "preacher's daughter" image, but she wasn't ready to shock the preacher, either. James Webster was a loving, understanding man of God, but he was also her father.

"I don't think I can take this," Mike groaned, dropping his head back on the seat. "Thank goodness we're already registered. I need a cold shower."

"Sheesh, why bother? They don't work."

"Cold water is more effective on the male body," Mike said, grinning despite the discomfort in his body. "Men and women are built differently."

"I know that," Callie said quickly.

"But in this case..." he said, squeezing her bottom, "it's like using a squirt gun on a forest fire."

Her saucy smile shot liquid pleasure through his veins. "I'll remember you said that."

"Please do." With a struggle, Mike brought himself under control as the limo pulled up in front of the hotel. He didn't want to face Callie's father with the obvious effect of their kiss still...obvious.

Reverend Webster waited in the lobby, waving as they walked inside. Callie took one look at the silver-haired man, threw herself into his welcoming embrace and burst into tears.

Panic crowded Mike's throat as he watched her cry. Was something wrong? She hadn't changed her mind about marrying him, had she?

"Now, now," James Webster soothed. "What's this all about?"

She sniffed. "I'm sorry. I'm just so happy."

"You're just like your mother. She cried, too."

"Don't fuss yerself, Calliope," a gruff voice said from behind them, and Callie jumped.

"Curdgeon?"

Curdgeon Post twisted his worn hat in his hands. "Yer man invited me. Hope you don't mind."

With lightning speed Callie's face went from tearful to delighted. She whirled and gave Mike a kiss before hugging Curdgeon. "I'm so glad you could come. Have you met my father?"

"We've been talkin'. He's got some sense fer a man of the cloth."

"Great. You know, I'm starved. Let's have some lunch."

The afternoon wedding was as perfect as if they'd spent months planning it, though in some ways it didn't seem real to Callie. She'd dreamed of this day so many times, she kept pinching herself to be sure it was really happening.

She repeated the words after her father, saying "I do" as she looked into Mike's brown eyes. Then came the cold metal of the ring sliding over her finger. A simple gold band, because she never wanted to take it off.

Soon everyone was laughing and crying, the way people got at weddings.

"I couldn't be happier," Mike's mother whispered. "I always thought of you as a daughter. Now it's official."

Callie hastily blotted tears before Ross and Dono-

van pulled her away into "congratulation" kisses.
Mike didn't look too happy about their exuberance,
but he dealt with it better than he'd handled their innocent flirting.

The whole group ate a fancy dinner at the hotel
restaurant. She smiled and blinked at the frequent
flashing of cameras, and a long time later Mike carried
her across the threshold of their suite.

"I wanted to do this hours ago," he murmured,
kissing her throat. "If they hadn't been family, I
would have told them to take a hike."

Callie swallowed.

She didn't know a lot about wedding-night protocol.
Were they supposed to just fall on each other like
love-starved rabbits? Or did a bride and groom go
through a ritual before they got undressed?

"Tired?" Mike asked.

"No...well, a little." She laughed self-consciously
and fidgeted with her wedding ring. "It's been a
crazy—"

"Vacation?" he suggested, smiling faintly.

"Right, vacation," Callie agreed with a smile.

Biting her lip, she adjusted Mike's tie, aware of his
intent gaze.

One of them had to make a move, but it was all so
planned. Artificial. They both knew what came next,
and Mike seemed so big, standing there in his suit and
tie. The rose boutonniere didn't fit his masculine image, and she turned to look around the suite. It was a
grand, fancy room with a private hot tub and fireplace.

"It's nice," she muttered.

"I wanted the best for you."

Mike's hand slid around her waist, stroking intimately over her tummy. Warmth built beneath his fingers and Callie swayed.

"I... Should we go to bed?" she suggested, no longer uncertain.

"Great idea." He kissed her lightly, then picked up a box from the bureau. "I got something for you to wear...something special."

It was a beautifully wrapped package, with pale peach paper and lace ribbon, and her stomach sank. She'd already gotten something special to wear, darn it. This was her wedding night and she didn't want Mike's idea of a virginal nightgown getting in the way. But his face was so loving and happy, she couldn't refuse.

"Use the bathroom," Mike said, giving her another lingering kiss. "I'll be waiting."

Waiting...swell. Callie took the package into the luxurious bathroom and stared at it for a full five minutes. She knew what was inside—one of those white, chiffony bridal sets. A long time ago she might have chosen something like that, but not now, and not for Mike.

Reluctantly she unwrapped the paper. A sea of tissue paper greeted her.

"Get it over with," Callie muttered.

She pushed the paper aside and her eyes widened. Not white, but black. And there wasn't much of it.

Lifting the gown, she shook out the gossamer folds. Though floor length, the sheer fabric didn't weigh a lot. Narrow insets of opaque silk were located in strategic locations, but they'd mostly draw attention, rather than conceal.

No lace.

Highly revealing.

A classy sort of erotic nightgown. *Very* sexy. She couldn't have gotten anything better herself.

Callie leaned against the counter and started laughing. It seemed Mike had the right idea after all.

She was laughing?

Mike clenched the neck of a champagne bottle and stared at the bathroom door. He didn't know what he'd expected, but he hadn't expected laughter.

Damn.

It had seemed such a good idea at the time. He'd hunted up a fancy boutique, then he had only looked at nightgowns *he*—as a man—wanted to see Callie wearing. Actually, he didn't want her to wear anything, and the gown he'd chosen was as close to naked as she could get while still technically wearing something.

The idea was to let Callie know how much he wanted and needed her—as a sensual, beautiful woman. But maybe he should have listened to the saleswoman and gotten something a little more... discreet.

It was their wedding night, after all. She probably had something more romantic in mind, than wearing a black, see-through nightgown.

"Er...Callie...? You don't have to wear it if you don't want. I won't mind." *At least not much.* He figured she wouldn't be wearing a nightgown for long, so more fabric one way or the other didn't matter.

"Coming."

The champagne bottle hit the floor as Callie strolled out, her bright hair glowing as it tumbled around her shoulders. The gown swirled around her body in a black mist, teasing him, revealing and concealing as she moved. But better than anything else was the beguiling smile on her face.

This was a confident woman. A seductress. A lady who knew what she wanted—and was about to get it.

"I think one of us is overdressed," Callie said, walking toward him.

"I know it isn't you," he murmured with a throaty laugh. "So it must be me."

She tugged his robe open and pushed it from his shoulders. Her fingers burned a trail down his bare chest, but he caught her hand before she reached her destination. If she touched him there, the evening would be over a lot faster than he had in mind.

"Mike?"

Cupping her face, Mike gazed into Callie's sweet, seductive eyes. "I love you," he said softly. "Thank you for coming to Alaska."

"My pleasure."

Mike grinned and lifted her high into his arms. "Not yet, Mrs. Fitzpatrick. But soon...very soon."

Callie pulled his head down for a long kiss, their mouths meeting in a sweet caress of love and laughter and passion, all mixed-up together.

"I've been thinking about our honeymoon," she breathed into her husband's mouth.

"Yeah?"

"What makes you think I'll let you out of this suite?"

Mike chuckled and laid her down on the mattress. "Well, they do have room service here."

"Then who needs Paris?"

Epilogue

Mike waved at his wife as she came down the porch steps. At eight months pregnant, she moved slower than normal, but only because he kept nagging about her being careful.

"I could have gotten that," he scolded as she handed him a cup of coffee.

"I know." Callie kissed him. "Do we have enough wood for the winter yet? We wouldn't want to run short."

"Just about." Mike took a sip of his coffee and chuckled. The firewood he'd chopped during their unusual courtship had lasted for two and a half winters, and she still loved to tease him about it.

"Can you take some time out for brunch?"

"Mmm, yes." He put his arm around Callie as they walked back inside. The scent of caramel and bacon surrounded him and he inhaled happily. His wife spoiled him shamefully. He'd slept in after a late flight the night before, and now she'd fixed his favorite meal.

Their two-year-old son sat on the floor, contentedly playing with the wooden airplane his grandfather Webster had sent for his birthday. At the sight of his mother he waved and blew a wet kiss.

"He's so beautiful," Callie said, her eyes soft.

Mike sat down on a chair and pulled her into his lap. "That's because he looks like you."

"Flatterer. You just want extra pancakes."

"Actually, I was thinking about..." He whispered into her ear and she laughed.

"That's how we got this little bundle." Callie patted her rounded stomach. "Remember?"

Remember? He'd never forget that frosty winter morning. She'd surprised him with breakfast in bed— caramel pecan pancakes, of course—then she'd shamelessly seduced him. Not that he had any reluctance in being seduced; she just did it so well, it was always a treat.

He certainly didn't mind mornings any longer. On the days he had to fly early, Callie always woke him up an hour ahead of time...to get some horizontal exercise together. Mike grinned, thinking of a few times he'd been late despite the extra hour.

"What are you snickering about?"

"I wasn't snickering, I was thinking about my alarm clock."

"You mean Harry? Just think, in a month we'll have another little screamer to wake you up. That should wipe the grin off your face."

Mike pinched her bottom and she yelped. "I don't mean our son, I meant my insatiable wife."

Callie gave Mike an admonishing look, then spoiled

it by laughing again. She hadn't thought she could love him any more, yet every day proved her wrong. Whether they were talking, or making love, or just taking a walk together, every moment held something special.

He'd even embraced fatherhood with boundless enthusiasm, taking more than his share of diapering duty and midnight walks with a teething baby. They'd decided on three kids, though Mike had hinted he wouldn't object to having more. Callie was considering it—she loved being a mommy. But she also wanted time for the two of them.

"Happy, Mrs. Fitzpatrick?" Mike murmured, his breath tickling her ear.

"Very."

"Good. Then after we eat, you can take pity on your poor husband and rub liniment on his aching muscles. I chopped a lot of wood to keep us warm next winter."

Callie raised one eyebrow. "You only worked for half an hour."

"Then you'll have to find something else that's aching. I'm sure if you put your mind to it, you'll figure out what it is."

She gave him an intimate caress. "I've got the picture, but we'll have to wait until Harry takes his afternoon nap—the price of parenthood. Everyone has to pay."

Mike groaned. "If I don't get help soon, I may need medical attention."

"Then it's a good thing you enticed that doctor into taking over the Kachelak Clinic three years ago. The poor man didn't have a chance against your fetish for being overprotective."

"I wanted you to be safe." Mike stroked Callie's

tummy. She became more beautiful with each day, and he loved touching the visible evidence of their bond. "I love you so much," he breathed. "So damned much."

"It took you long enough, Michael Fitzpatrick."

He looked into her merry green eyes, filled with love, and smiled. Callie was his fantasy lady, now and forever. Lucky for him, she'd turned out to be real.

* * * * *

Look for HANNAH GETS A HUSBAND, the next book in Julianne Morris's series, BRIDAL FEVER, coming in May 2000 from Silhouette Romance!

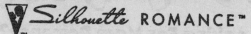

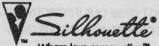

Looking For More Romance?

Visit Romance.net

Look us up on-line at: http://www.romance.net

Check in daily for these and other exciting features:

Hot off the press

View all current titles, and purchase them on-line.

What do the stars have in store for you?

Horoscope

Hot deals

Exclusive offers available only at Romance.net

Plus, don't miss our interactive quizzes, contests and bonus gifts.

PWEB

Look Who's Celebrating Our 20ᵗʰ Anniversary:

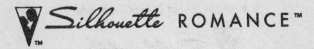

"Happy 20ᵗʰ birthday, Silhouette. You made the writing dream of hundreds of women a reality. You enabled us to give [women] the stories [they] wanted to read and helped us teach [them] about the power of love."

—*New York Times* bestselling author
Debbie Macomber

"I wish you continued success, Silhouette Books.... Thank you for giving me a chance to do what I love best in all the world."

—International bestselling author
Diana Palmer

"A visit to Silhouette is a guaranteed happy ending, a chance to touch magic for a little while.... It refreshes and revitalizes and makes us feel better.... I hope Silhouette goes on forever."

—Award-winning bestselling author
Marie Ferrarella

Silhouette ROMANCE™

Soldiers of Fortune...prisoners of love.

*Back by popular demand, international bestselling
author* **Diana Palmer**'s *daring and
dynamic* Soldiers of Fortune *return!*

*Don't miss these unforgettable
romantic classics in our
wonderful 3-in-1
keepsake collection.
Available in April 2000.**

And look for a **brand-new** *Soldiers of Fortune* tale in May.
Silhouette Romance presents the next book in
this riveting series:

MERCENARY'S
WOMAN

(SR #1444)

She was in danger and he fought to protect her. But
sweet-natured Sally Johnson dreamed of spending forever
in Ebenezer Scott's powerful embrace. Would she walk
down the aisle as this tender mercenary's bride?

Then in January 2001, look for THE WINTER SOLDIER
in Silhouette Desire!

*Available at your favorite retail outlet.
Also available on audio from Brilliance.

Silhouette®

™ *Where love comes alive*™

VIRGIN BRIDES

Join
Silhouette Romance
as the New Year brings new
virgin brides down the aisle!

On Sale December 1999
THE BRIDAL BARGAIN
by Stella Bagwell (SR #1414)

On Sale February 2000
WAITING FOR THE WEDDING
by Carla Cassidy (SR #1426)

On Sale April 2000
HIS WILD YOUNG BRIDE
by Donna Clayton (SR #1441)

Watch for more **Virgin Brides** stories from
your favorite authors later in 2000!

VIRGIN BRIDES
only from

Silhouette®
Where love comes alive™

Available at your favorite retail outlet.

Visit us at www.romance.net   SRVB00